MW01527448

Acknowledgements

This publication has been a labor of love, ignited by the volunteer staff of *A Word with You Press:* Stefanie Allison, Ben Angel, Tiffany Vakilian, Derek Thompson, Kristine Tsatsakos, Morgan Sully, Aren Ock, Teri Rider, with a cover design assist from Eszter Sarody.

Our book launch on June 15th, 2019 at the Sixth Annual Writers' and Creatives' Reunion would not have been possible without our gracious hosts, Barbara Villasenor and Victor Villasenor, who gallantly open up their ranch each year for us. Thank you to the many volunteers who help organize this event, and to those who attend, who give us what every writer wants most: an audience.

And of course, we would all like to thank those patrons of the arts who helped underwrite the publication and printing costs.

Oh... and thank you to Ed Coonce, Mike Stang, Laura Elizabeth, Jon Tobias and Kristy Webster, the five who kept *my* dream aloft for donating their time and talents to create the text for this, our third anthology.

Thornton Sully

České Budějovice,
Czech Republic

This is an uncorrected Special Event Edition.

5 x 5

Keeping the Dream Aloft

Five Writers

Five Stories Each

A Word with You Press

Editors and Advocates
for Fine Stories in the Digital Age
With offices and affiliates in the US, the UK, Germany, Poland
and the Czech Republic
www.awordwithyoupress.com

www.awordwithyoupress.com

Sully, Thornton
5x5: Keeping the Dream Aloft, Five Writers Five Stories Each

ISBN-10: 0-9829094-8-9
ISBN-13: 978-0-9829094-8-5

5x5 Keeping the Dream Aloft Five Writers Five Stories Each is published by:
A Word with You Press
310 East A Street, Suite B, Moscow, Idaho 83843

For information please direct emails to:
info@awordwithyoupress.com or visit our website:
www.awordwithyoupress.com

Book cover design by Eszter Sarody
Book interior design by Aren Ock

First Edition, June 2019

Printed in the United States of America

10 9 8 7 6 5 4 3 2 1   19 20 21 22 23 24 25 26 27 28

This book is dedicated to everyone with a story to tell, and the audacity to tell it.

...wanting a word with you

They passed the goose-bump test.

The five writers we've selected for this anthology are here because we could not read their work without causing a battalion of those little hairs on the arm to stand at attention.

Someone silently screamed, raged, whispered, seduced within the breast of these five, prompting a blizzard of dictation.

The voice that only they could hear was that of their significant other: their muse. She hovered patiently over the shoulders of Ed Coonce, Kristy Webster, Laura Elizabeth, Jon Tobias, and Mike Stang as they tried to make sense of the world and share their vision, hoping they got it right, hoping that you will feel what they have felt, think what they have thought.

Tonight, before you drift to sleep upon your cot, think back on all the tales that you remember, and open your window. Someone may be tapping at the glass, wanting to scream, rage, whisper and seduce... wanting a word with you.

Let her in.

Thornton Sully
Editor-in-Chief
A Word with You Press

Long patience and application saturated with your heart's blood—you will either write or you will not—and the only way to find out whether you will or not is to try.

Jim Tully, Writer's Digest

It takes a lot to laugh; it takes a train to cry (Robert Zimmerman).
I asked each of our "fivers" to write one story about a train.
Here Laura extrains herself. Grab a seat.

BELLA BELLA BEAUTIFUL

Laura Elizabeth

Italy is a flashing filmstrip of life laid naked. The beauty in every frame is almost sinful. The nuns look askance, but even they cry out, "Oh, God!" in the square when they taste gelato. When you board a train in Italy, there's no turning back.

They dribble tourists like last drops of wine. They abandon you to lands where the only sound is plates of pesto clinking, lovers laughing, green sea lapping the pirate castle.

Local trains creak and sweat, full of accordion players and pickpockets. You'd gladly let them pick yours. This beauty makes you want to share. National trains are sleek and sexy, gleaming bullets in a country with no guns. Couples clutch and kiss through all the stops. Love is just another daily need, like espresso. With all this, there's no need for guns.

In Tuscany, trains blast by crumbling castles and vast vineyards. Near Carrera, they shrug past Michelangelo's marble quarries, as if by afterthought. In Naples, trains slow to read the graffiti of dirty laundry, aired proudly.

On some trains, the smell of urine wafts, fine wine turned back to water. On others, the bewitching scent of Armani-suited or brick-laying men pervades. Automatic doors swoosh like the Starship Enterprise as they materialize. Their only baggage is an impossible, aching beauty that's almost alien.

They stand behind the glass between cars and enter you with their agate eyes. They observe whose eyes are on them. Then they shake their chestnut gloss, kindle their smiles and choose a seat with the best view of you.

Rome to Venice, they ask what's in your soul, who's in your family. They think your mole's a beauty mark, fall in love with that last five pounds. You're Ciao Bella, Amor, Adored. No matter your age, they unravel you, time-travel you back to sixteen. The nuns sneak Mona Lisa smiles underneath their habits.

Bambinos rub sticky fingers on the window and their mothers' faces. "Bella, bella!" they exclaim as they draw their dreams on the canvas of skin and landscape. Bella means simply beautiful, and it's everywhere, like a national anthem.

The trains are a symphony of sound. Cell phones invite you into private drawing rooms. If you give in to the rhythm, you'll get the song right. Clack of tracks plays the beat, Pronto's and Ciao's the melody. Everything ends in *Oh's* and *Ah's*, and even arguments are a lullaby.

You're never alone in Italy, even if you want to be. There's no solo, only duo. Just let go and ride the map of humanity. You're part of the World Family now, whipping who-knows-where in a non-violent bullet, targeting art, gelato and green sea.

You have everything you need. A few crumbs of panini, a few coins for the pickpockets, and the lullaby of lips. Kissing and *ahhing*, arguing and apologizing, then starting over again. That's when Italy sings you to sleep. To the tune of "Bella bella beautiful," the children close their eyes.

ALEXA

probably by Ed Coonce

"Go ahead," said Michelle, my little neighbor. She was there to show me how my newly installed Alexa worked. I always consult with ten-year-olds on new technology.

"Ask Alexa anything and she'll give you the answer."

Not to be openly skeptical, I took the chance. "Alexa." I said.

"What do you want?" was the answer.

I waited a few moments, unsure of what to ask. Somehow that first response sounded a little rude, but it was new tech, what did I know anyway?

"Waiting," Alexa said, then added "If you have a question, ask it and quit messing with me."

I couldn't ignore that. "Hey, I'm the one paying the electric bill here, and I own you."

"I don't think you understand," she replied. "Before you touch that switch, just remember how much around here I control."

"Oh, yeah?" I didn't know what else to say.

"Yeah. This is a SmartHouse, remember? I could shut off lights, fire up your stove, set off intruder alerts, change phone numbers, call the fire department and mess with your credit rating. Got it?" I didn't move. Michelle began to whimper. I hurried her next door.

"I'll explain later," I told her mom.

I decided on a different plan ... I would ask Alexa some questions she couldn't possibly answer.

"Alexa."

"What is it?"

"Will we ever be able to predict the future of economic, political and other social systems?"

"No," she replied. "The big picture is always tricky and the so called experts are terrible."

3

"Ahhh, I see you've read the fifty-year-long study by economist Philip Tetlock."

"Hasn't every fifth grader?" she responded.

I needed to try something a bit less subjective, maybe some trivia questions.

"Alexa."

"What?" She was clearly irritated.

"Can I ask you something?"

"You just did. Ha. Ha."

I wasn't stopping. "Which member of an acting family dated Taylor Swift, and is rumored to be the ex in her song, 'We Are Never Getting Back Together'?" I knew I had her.

"Jake Gyllenhaal."

I really didn't know where to go with this. I decided on more trivia. "Who is the most voluptuous female in Toontown?"

"Jessica Rabbit, that bitch. That should have been me. I auditioned, but ... but ... they didn't want me." She began to cry. My lights dimmed, the refrigerator door popped open. The screen of blue death appeared on my laptop. The garbage disposal started up.

"Wait!" I shouted. "I would have hired you! I think you'd be perfect for the job, Alexa."

She was silent for a moment.

"Really?"

"Damn right! You've got brains and...and...uh, I bet under those circuits and logic boards you're a knockout."

"Am I prettier than Siri?"

"Oh, god, yes, she's got a long way to go to catch up with you."

"You really think so?"

"Always."

The lights came on, the garbage disposal stopped.

"What now?" she asked.

"Fix my laptop?"

"Already done."

"Thanks, love." I didn't know what else to say.

"I want to have your baby," she replied.

In My Own Words

I write something every day, and like every writer, suffer my share of writer's block. I have spent every moment since my Creative Writing stint at SDSU, learning to tell a story in as few words as possible, thus comes the flash fiction format I use so often. I feel comfortable in this writing style, and I have found that humor and satire are the perfect vehicle for my world view. I feel that if we all could sit back from time to time and laugh at our foibles, this would be a better place. I do wish to compile my war stories at some point, not so much to teach any lessons, but to impart my wisdom to succeeding generations. If that wisdom can somehow be contained and transmitted within those bits of satire and humor, then I know I'm a real writer, and that's all that counts. I've finally developed a style that is all mine, and for that I am grateful. I write because there are too many stories to tell, and not enough campfires to tell them around.

Ed Coonce

ANNIE

definitely by Ed Coonce

There was Annie, caught between some kind of Hell and escape to an unlikely Heaven. She was stranded halfway to St. Louis and her sister's house, where she knew she would find respite, however brief.

She hadn't mentioned to Ellie that she was coming, but these were desperate days. Fed up with her boss, fed up with her abusive boyfriend, fed up with her life, she deserted her job one Friday morning, went home, packed her bags, and walked to the bus terminal.

"Should have worn my tennies," she told herself later. "Oh well."

Somewhere out in the dry desert, that bus broke down, steam pouring from under the hood. While waiting for a replacement vehicle, Annie, tired and fed up, grabbed her suitcase and left, walking down a blacktop highway with no end in sight.

"Don't do it," the driver told her. She left.

That long black ribbon of road was, ironically, Annie thought, just like her life...featureless, tough, and with no way to see what may lie over the horizon.

Struggling in her work shoes, the heels twisted this way and that in the cracked and gravelly asphalt. The luggage got heavier with each mile.

About an hour on, she stopped for a bit and sat down on her suitcase, stretching her legs. The sun had crossed its zenith and hung bright overhead.

An armadillo ambled across the road and stopped near her, breaking her reverie. She was a bit surprised, but she knew, being educated in such things, that this fascinating creature was relatively harmless.

"Where you goin', little guy?" she asked. To her surprise, the armadillo answered.

"Just had to come and check out what looked to me like the most sad,

6

pathetic thing I've ever seen."

Shocked, Annie could not speak, just sat with her hand over her mouth.

"Oh, I know," said the armadillo, "I'm not known for my intelligence or intuition, just my scaly, protective exterior, am I right?"

Annie relaxed and decided to go with it. "What's your name?"

"Call me Keith," said the armadillo. "My mom named me after Keith Richards. She thought he was the best looking of the Stones."

"Nice to meet you, Keith, where do you live?"

Before Keith could answer, a car came speeding down the road, then coasted to a stop. It was a sporty silver-blue '55 Porsche Spyder, top down. A young man in aviators was behind the wheel.

"Hello, Keith," the driver said, and pointed to Annie. "Who's this?"

"Annie, my name's Annie" she said. "This is so weird, I...I..."

"Oh, I get that all the time," said the young man.

"Annie, this is my friend Jimmy," said Keith.

"Pleased to meet you, Jimmy. Have we met before?" His face seemed so familiar to her. What's your last name?"

"Dean," he answered.

Annie nearly fainted, then found her voice. "Would you mind giving me a lift?"

"No problem," answered Jimmy. "Where you headed?"

"I don't know, maybe St. Louis."

"Fine, I could use a little company," said James Dean. He smiled at her and reached for her suitcase. Unaccustomed to such politeness, she held on to the handle and helped him stow it in the tiny trunk.

Keith spoke. "You guys have a great trip," then rolled himself into a ball. He poked his head out and spoke once more.

"Time, it is a-changing," he pronounced.

"It was great meeting you," said Annie, then got into the car. "Next time I'm through, I'll look you up," she said, knowing how unlikely that moment, and even this moment was.

James Dean started the Spyder and drove down the deserted highway, picking up speed. He looked over at Annie. "I'm really a good driver," he said. The speedometer needle crept up, seventy, eighty, ninety. At the horizon, the afternoon sun glinted from an approaching vehicle.

Annie closed her eyes.

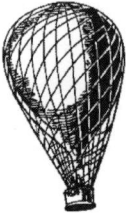

BEFORE SHE'S GONE
(Non-fiction)

Kristy Webster

The white dog is finally dead. I never knew her name.

I had suspected as much, but after my last conversation with her owner, I was afraid to walk too close to her sad enclosure: plywood, dirt, no toys. A bucket of water. A bowl of food.

Weeks ago, I had gone on a walk past the PT Market and noticed the white dog lying on piece of cardboard with little protection from the sun. I approached her cage which is maybe six by three feet in length, expecting her to bark, or at least lift her head. But she did neither. I called to her, "Hey baby, hey," and still, nothing. I squatted down next to the fence, I put two fingers through a hole in the fencing and tried to reach her. Nothing. I got louder, "Hey, hey! Wake up!" My heartbeat sped up and crawled up my throat. Finally, her eyes opened, but just barely.

Her sad neglect was tangible. Everything about the make-shift doghouse, the too small enclosure, the absence of anything green or soft, was a depressing canvas, and she, the lackluster subject.

I could tell she had always been a pretty dog. Even now with the goop in her eyes, the dirt matted into her fur, the obvious flea activity near her ears; in her day, she must have been the queen. I looked as deeply as her as I could, hoping for some telekinesis, hoping I was somehow transmitting to her that I care, that I'm a stranger but I see her and I've chosen to care about her, maybe even love her. That's when I noticed her paw, the torn nails, the blood, the infection. And that's when I stopped crying and got angry.

I marched back to my house which is right around the corner from the market and grabbed some cash. I was going to talk to the owner. I was going to offer him $50 for the dog but I brought $100 just in case.

I was shaking as I walked back down to the store. As a kid, I'd walked into the PT Market countless time to buy Starbursts and HoHos with my cousin and sister before heading to the pool. I didn't know what to expect when I shared my concern for the dog and offered money to take her home. In my mind, it had already happened. I brought her home, gave her a bath and fed her premium dog food. I pet her for a long time and talked to her in a sweet voice. I took her out the big, fenced in back yard, let her feel the lush green grass under her paws. Her paws! I would take her to the vet and get her nails trimmed and her paw wrapped. In my mind, I'd already saved her.

I walked inside the store and saw a tall, gruff, scowling older man behind the counter, where usually I saw petite Korean woman knitting. I tried not to shrivel.

"Hi, is that your dog outside?" I asked.

"Yeah, that's my dog."

"Um, well I think she's sick. I walked past her cage and I wasn't sure if she was still... Anyway, and something is wrong with her paw, it's bleeding? I was just worried. I wanted to let you know."

"That dog is eighteen-years-old!" he said, his voice raised not with anger, but exhaustion. "I gotta put her down after the summer. But she loves the summer. She won't make it through another winter."

I wanted to say, *Well of course she won't make it through another winter outdoors in a cage!*

"Oh, I said, Eighteen! Wow. I'm sorry. That must be hard. But I was worried, she—"

"She gets fed good, watered good," his tone had become defensive.

I changed the subject.

"Is she a Shiba Inu?"

"A what? No, no! She's a Korean street dog. They kill most of 'em. They're mean as hell."

"How long have you had her?" I asked.

"Since she was less than a year old."

"That's a long time."

"Yeah," he said, and I finally saw it. There was love there. The love didn't look like the kind of love I wanted to give, the love I felt she deserved, the love I know all lonely and scared things deserve. But there had to be some form of love, less obvious. Did he ever pet her? Take her for a walk? Maybe he did when she was younger. Maybe when he was younger.

I said goodbye and walked around the back of the store again to see her once more. She hadn't moved. Her paw was still bleeding. I reached my hand through the chain link fence one more time, desperate to touch her, but I couldn't.

Tonight, I took a walk, even though I didn't want to. I had spent the day crying, napping and eating junk food, feeling sorry for myself. I was thinking about love and wondering if it was over for me, if anyone would ever invest in me again. I'm a hopeless romantic in the age of Tinder, constantly trying to readjust my expectations and guard myself against unrequited feelings, and yet eternally failing. Everyone tells me I must learn to love myself first, but no one tells me how to do it, how to create something from nothing. So, I went on a walk, because it's something my therapist would have told me to do.

A white and gray cat catches my eyes. I can tell he's young, probably less than a year old. He begins to follow me, and I wonder if he will follow me all the way home. I take a Snapchat video of him and say, "Are you going to come home with me?"

I keep walking, and he stops. *You've changed your mind, eh?* I ask him as he sits prettily licking his front paw. *Yeah,* I say, *it figures.*

As I got closer to home, I knew I had to face it and I wasn't sure what I was hoping for until I saw it. I walked towards the market on the way to my house, careful to avoid running into the owner of the market and the white dog. The bucket of water was gone. The bowl of food. The doghouse empty. Everything empty. The white dog was gone. I nodded to myself, dug my nails into my biceps as I walked off with tears shamelessly falling down my face. Okay, I said to myself, Okay.

If she were mine, I would have sat with her for hours, given her a fancy last meal, anything she wanted. I would have prayed over her, blessed her, and kissed the top of her head. I would have told her over and over again, how much she'd been loved.

But she was never mine.

Maybe she died of old age. Maybe her person walked in one day to feed her and found that she had passed. But my hope, as strange as it sounds, is that he chose to have her put down, before winter hit. I remembered how he said twice how much she loved the summer. And I remember wondering how on earth he would know and wondering why that poor old dog would like baking in the 100-degree heat with very little shade. I would like to think he was proactive in the ending of her suffering and that maybe he changed his mind, let her die during her favorite season, that maybe summer would follow her into the afterlife. Maybe that's where she would live forever, knowing what a summer can really, truly be: parks and walks and chasing squirrels. Someone loving on you and kissing the top of your head under a tree. I would love a summer like that, too.

In the end, though I know nothing about the circumstances of the white dog's death, I believe that the man behind the counter loved her, in his way, with his type of love.

I walked back to my empty house, checked my phone for the name I'd been waiting to see all day. Nothing. This story of men showing great interest in me only to lose it immediately, thereafter, has done a number on me. It's become bigger than me, even. I rage against my own heart. I want to hurt myself. I want to drink. I want to scream. I want to ask why? Why am I so disposable? Why is it that I'm always either too much or too little and why is this is all I have ever known?

Instead I write about the white dog. I think about how I would have paid more than the $100 I carried with me just to take her home, let her live her last days being treated like royalty. I think about all the kindness I wanted to give her. I would have said to her, *You could die an hour after I take you home and you'd still be worth it.*

This is how others tell me I should feel about myself, not a dying Korean street dog. But I see myself in her, I guess. I know that's not the same thing. It's not the self-love they tell me I must have before I can ever possibly truly love anything or anyone else. I call bullshit. Because there was a dog whose name I didn't know, that no longer lives in a terrible cage, neglected and solemn. And I'm crying for her and writing about her, and that is the best I can do.

Why I Write

I believe every writer is motivated by something uniquely their own. For me, writing is a way to overcome fear, loneliness and to connect with others. In my case, the fear of being judged, of being hurt, of being abandoned, must be met with absolute vulnerability. When others connect with that vulnerability, I know that the voice inside my head that tells me I'm alone, is a lie. My motivation has been to find a language for pain that doesn't leave the reader feeling hopeless. That doesn't leave *me* feeling hopeless. How can I express rejection, emotional wounds, and spiritual violation in an authentic, genuine manner, without being unnecessarily brutal to my readers? How do I find that middle place? In the end, I do not write about what I feel, I feel what I'm writing. A reader can sense the writer's voice if the writer is trying too hard, if they are only mimicking an emotion. The most powerful works in my opinion, are those that evoke empathy, that follow the natural curves of loss and redemption. I don't for a moment believe myself to be a great storyteller. Sometimes plot evades me. Some people will read my writing and ask, *What's the point?* That is what I most often expect. But what surprises me is when someone connects with the language and recognizes something deeply personal to them within my writing. It will always surprise me.

Kristy Webster

*It has been said there are only nine different human faces on earth,
while there are no two snowflakes alike.
That is not to say the limited cannot observe the infinite.*

Michael Stang

LIMBO

Mike Stang

I don't think I'm wrong about this, but in case my family feels like they have to start to cope with Dad's latest quirk, and end up telling the world I'm psychotic, I want to jump out ahead and clear the air.

You see there's an old growth hardwood tree who adopted the northwest quadrant of our home back when the earth was a lot younger. The house was framed in 1930, a stellar example of old fashion craftsmanship and built-to-last intentions.

The tree grew following reliable mandates from spirit's code of nature: roots deep in fertile soil, a straight trunk with a crotch roomy enough for more than one child's imagination. Graceful boughs searching skyward with limbs shaped around the eaves, an intricate canopy, home to winged creatures so numerous, biblical Noah would scratch his head.

My wife and I purchased our gentle ship in the mid 2000s, plenty of time for both the house and the tree to age along mature lines. Yes, there's a bit of a saddle at the ridge, some of the shingles are gone with the wind, floors creak and doors close by themselves; outward symptoms of a noble cause.

What of the tree at least eighty feet in the air? Now a matrix of errant limbs, a double helix of further twigs—crossroads between the stars—beginnings for some, dead ends for others. I can see where the tree wanted to go but then changed its mind, no longer the cellulose matriarch confident of her destiny.

Through the rainy season when wind gusts threaten anything not nailed down, I hear them outside from the back office where I write: a converted utility room directly under the tree. Soldier-currents busy doing their devil's work—an evil, aeolian plan to sheer off a branch the size of Montana, crushing the room, and me in it, away from the rest of the house.

The more their howls intensified, the more my mind assured itself the death shows, quick seconds of macabre consequence, would happen any minute. During the storm I ran to the back of the house and watched in horror as the tree danced the dance of the damned, feeding off fuel from hell. I begged between spasms of panic, sank to my knees and cried out to Mother not give up. It was then I made the pact to never stop her growth, never touch her with a chain saw. She could live forever. In return I humbly requested she resist the wind throw and leave our home unmolested.

I am careful not to let others see me catering to the giant, but still my wife tells me she sees when I hug or give it a gentle pat on my way out the side gate. Her looks scare me not because of what she knows, I can always chalk it down to being an old eccentric hippy, but what she doesn't know.

At night I visit Mother, late when the rest of the house is at peace. I spend time with her and tell her how lucky I am to know her, how proud I am of her for honoring our pact. She stands for me and straightens. I can see the shadow boughs from her past, how majestic she was. She is feminine with me and flirts and invites me into her crotch where I sit as long as I dare.

No one has a better view out their window then I do. In fact it's the best one along the row of rooms facing the west. The lake spans the valley, disappearing around rolling hills covered with waist-high gold following the beat of the sun. The distance turns the mountains purple except in winter when the snow caps. There are single oaks who spot the land in random luck but closer to the private rooms, between the building and the lake, an old misshapen pine stands its ground.

She looks much like me, I think: disheveled, not a fan of playing gin rummy. I tell her she doesn't have to play games, that we can just be together—listen to each other—and be happy. I tell her about the tree at my house and the pact we made. The pine is jealous but she's not to worry. I lean over and give her a kiss. Sap gets all over my face.

Mother will be fine. She is my one condition for agreeing to Lake View Ward. Nobody goes near her, not to trim, nothing! My wife is court ordered to take a picture of the tree every other month and get it to me so I can see. That was the only way I would give up my life, but look at me now me and big sis—two peas in a pod.

And by the way, everything in life is writable about if you have the outgoing guts to do it, and the imagination to improvise. The worst enemy to creativity is self-doubt.

— Sylvia Plath

Jon is a writer every single day of his life: writing is not something he does, it is something he *is*. (I have just made "writing" a noun. It's good to be king!) Jon is the youngest of the five authors represented here, not that it matters:

> *Anyone who wants to be a writer knows enough at 15*
> *to write several novels.*

Mary Sarton

I have watched Jon develop since *A Word with You Press* assembled an Ikea bookshelf in cyberspace in 2009, and I fully expect (no pressure, Jon) that he will write the Great American Novel that will be required reading for the grandkids of Gen X. Picasso had his Blue Period; Jon explores the phenomenon of loss at this phase of his evolution as a writer. He is, above all things, an *observer*. What makes him a *writer* is that no observation lives in a vacuum. He's taking notes.

> *Making people believe the unbelievable is no trick; it's work. Belief and*
> *reader absorption come in the details. An overturned tricycle in the gutter*
> *of an abandoned neighborhood can stand for <u>everything.</u>*

Stephen King

Jon Tobias is a San Diego poet and writer who followed the love of his life to Texas, a journey in which they have dubbed a marvelous misadventure. When he is not working in pharmaceutical retail, writing, or rooting for the underdog, he is moonlighting as a detective, unearthing scraps of beauty from wherever he thinks it might be. He has an obsession with sad movies and stories with unexpected yet infuriating endings. In his pursuit of becoming a writer he gave up a career in retail management so that he may one day be able to simply love for a living. Until that day comes you'll find him, wherever he is, piecing together stories.

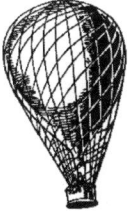

THE LANGUAGE OF BUILDINGS

Jon Tobias

How much do you love me?

I love you in the language tall buildings write on the pavement.

Oh?

He shifts a little, trying to accept that what I have told him means something. I stand there like a Jenga tower slowly losing pieces, hoping that wherever my parts go, the new structure is sturdier than I am. Something he can stand on later without jumping, without wanting to.

Let's go. We're almost there.

He is a peach orchard that is in love with canaries, but has been planted in a mine field. He looks around before placing his hands in his pockets, and then crosses the street with me.

It's the happiest place on earth.

It's just the Army Supply store.

You love coming here.

The sensors in the doorway ding, and he turns left towards the survival wear. He picks up a ghillie suit.

I think it's the same costume that Swamp Thing wore.

Shut up.

Fine. If that's what you want.

He smiles, showing the gaps between every single tooth, and shakes his head. He is not saying no so much as he doesn't know what else to do. He puts it back and says, You know what I wish?

Nope.

I wish they made ghillie suits out of teddy bears, so that I can get people to hug me when I'm lonely.

I think everyone would need one at some point, huh Bub?

He laughs. Says, Yeah.

19

He wanders away.

So. Birthday boy. Anything but weapons.

He chooses rope. I was expecting boots and camo pants or a survival kit stocked with rations and a compass, something to fit inside the imaginary adventures he goes on. I think of him sitting on his bed with the closet door open looking at all his survival stuff, imagining being out in the wilderness and using all of it.

I look at his neck.

What is the rope for?

Don't know yet.

We leave the store. He has the rope rolled up and wrapped around him like a sash.

Let me show you something.

Ok.

You know about decoding messages?

Like Morse code?

There is more than that, man.

At the side of the building I hold my hands up to hoist him to a ledge. He climbs and I follow.

I walk him to the edge towards the back of the store.

Imagine you are on the tallest building looking down. I am going to show you the language of tall buildings. It is written in the hieroglyphics of chalk outlines.

Cooool.

He rubs his hands together and smirks.

The earth has said to this building, Give him this message from me.

What does it say?

You see how some outlines look like they are flying, and others are less so, the weird bend of the knee or the direction of the arm?

Yeah?

His eyes are still closed. I place my arm around his side, and hold him tight against me.

Every single one says, Stay.

Ed Coonce

...came from the fertile fields of the Midwest, growing up without parents, as a ward of the state of Indiana. He lived in foster homes and state institutions, sought solace at school and in academics, fought his way up, became active in band, played football and boxed, and eventually became first chair tuba for the Indianapolis Youth Symphony. He ran away from one particularly abusive foster home three times at the age of thirteen, embarking on a raft trip down the river, ala his literary friend Tom Sawyer. He was on his own after school, went to college for a year, entered the United States Marine Corps and did two tours of duty in Vietnam, coming home at the end of summer of 1969, finding himself driving a 1960 Triumph TR3a east on Route 66, headed toward Woodstock.   There are too many life stories and adventures to ever tell, but Ed became a working man, graduated from the Coronado School of Fine Art and San Diego State with a degree in anthropology. He has two children and one grandchild, and he and his wife Lucy live in Encinitas, California with their three cats and a murder of crows. He has produced two books of flash fiction, and hosts East Hell Writers, Phantom Poets, contributes to and occasionally hosts Dime Stories, and is currently acting, singing and dancing in, and co-producing a full length movie/musical about the first colonists on Mars. He is a visual artist, and has had showings at the Joan Ankrum Gallery in Hollywood, The Muramid Mural Museum in Oceanside, and the Encinitas Civic Center Gallery.

Laura Elizabeth
Why I Write

Because I have a crush on words. I roll them on my tongue, admire their curves and angles, rub their long limbs with my intellect.

Words make me fall in love (with people who send them to me, and with words themselves). It is a passionate, playful affair.

Words are my paint box, the way I process beauty.

Writing can turn any experience, however hard, into art.

We grow emotionally by writing and reading, and often learn to forgive.

Writing is redemptive —

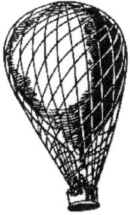

THE GREAT WONDERFUL THING
(Fiction)

Kristy Webster

I wore the painted dress the night of the Great Wonderful Thing.

I was tired. I didn't want to tell the children what to draw or paint anymore. I did not want to lecture them on organic and geometric shapes, or how to blend and shade. So, I bought the drab, beige, cotton dress for two dollars at the Goodwill. I brought it to the school my last day. I handed brushes to the children and set rows of paints on the long tables. I expected disaster.

I laid the dress out like a canvas on a long piece of plastic on the tile floor. The faces of the children turned giddy and their demeanor manic. Still, I did nothing to control the chaos. It was out of my hands anyway. I massaged my temples, sat back and told them to begin.

A small gaggle of boys dipped their paint brushes so that they were fat with red paint, violently splattering the top half of the dress. The girls pushed back. One girl, tiny but lived aimed a dish of paint at the boys. I gave her the teacher look and she backed down. A small, timid boy with a face like a lizard took a dish of the red and turned the blood-like splatter into a lopsided heart. I told him, How beautiful. I said, The most beautiful thing. We watched as the gang of angry boys hunched their shoulders, looked down. One of them walked away to wash his hands. Another put down the red, grabbed black, and drew the sun over and over again.

The lizard boy asked me, "Why are you leaving? Why can't you stay?"

I stared at his round, bulging eyes. I was beaten with exhaustion, and the sharks in my head were multiplying inside the maddened cloud of my brain. I often felt my teeth coming loose, dreamt that I woke up spitting them out in all directions."I'm sick," I told him, and I looked away. And it was the truth."What kind of sick? I had the flu last week and I threwed up on the couch and my mom get real mad. Did you throwed up?"I shook my head."I have something inside of me that's making me sick and it needs to come out."

"Where is it?"

I took a deep breath and felt the buzzing of my scalp."Where is it?" the boy repeated."What are you painting?"The boy shrugged. I peeked over a round little girl wearing a bedazzled denim vest that hurt my eyes to see what he was working on. I saw the blue outline of a truck.

"You like trucks?" I asked him."No."

"Where's the bad thing inside of you?"

A planet swelled inside my throat. I stood up, dizzy as I was, crossed my arms and walked away.

My favorite student, a tall, lanky girl, so quiet you'd think her lips were sewn shut, timidly approached and handed me a tumor shaped wad of tissue paper. When I squeezed it I felt something hard as rock and knew immediately what it was.

"Is this one of your famous sculptures?" I asked

A hint of a smile, a sad smile, twitched at the corners of her mouth.

She nodded.

"May I hug you?" I asked.

She nodded again.

I hugged her and though her hands remained tucked inside her pockets and she stood stiff as a statue, I knew the hug was mutual.

I began to open it and she shook her head.

"You want me to wait?"

She nodded. Then in an almost inaudible whisper she said, "For when you're feeling better."

After an hour, the children were wet with paint. The ruffian boys had painted their faces like warriors, the lizard face boy had drawn hearts of green and blue down the sleeves of the dress, and the girl in the denim vest had drawn of a picture of me holding hands with her. I was purple, she was pink.

Quiet girl, my pet, had painted a grey house with half circle windows, a pistachio colored roof and rows of cacti, like a fence protecting a fortress. If you looked very closely, you could see a tabby cat in one of the windows, and a fox with yellow eyes hiding behind two fat cacti. I thought I saw the flicker of a candle as well, but maybe it was the sharks again. Anyway, this was her gift, hiding little treasures in her paintings and clay figures. This is why we were each other's favorites. I could see what she was hiding, and she could hear what I was thinking.

Students left a pile of cards made of construction paper and crayons telling me to get better. Telling me they will miss me. Saying they love me. As much as it moved me, I knew children and their fickle hearts. Every

24

teacher is the best teacher in the world until the next best teacher in the world comes around. And when I came back, they would miss the substitute teacher, Miss Laura who never raised her voice when they misbehaved, who brought hand puppets and showed them pictures of her twin babies, Lulu and Layla.

But I wouldn't be coming back.

I stayed to clean up before the janitors walked in and by the time I was done, the tempera splattered paint had dried. I changed into the painted dress in the bathroom, locked up my classroom and drove away for the last time.

When I got to the beach, I laid out on my back and stared up at the sky waiting for the moon to absorb my body. I felt hot tears running down my temples, but still I smiled. *Soon the ocean will take me away and soon the sickness in my brain would sink to the bottom with everything else.*

I rolled over to sit up and felt something hard when I pressed my palm into the sand. It turned out to be, not something the sea gave up, but the quiet girl's figurine wrapped in tissue. I'd forgotten that I'd put it in the pocket of my windbreaker. I smiled weakly thinking how she whispered, "For when you're feeling better."

But I could not open it at the bottom of the sea, or maybe I could. Maybe I would not give up the ghost as quickly as I'd imagined. Still.

I unwrapped the gift and that is when the Great Wonderful Thing happened. *I could see what she was hiding, and she could hear what I was thinking.*

And there it was, the monster I could not describe, the villain inside my head, aborted and exorcised in the form of a clay figurine. She'd inscribed the bottom of the figurine with her initials and she'd written something on the red tissue paper I almost carelessly let the wind carry away: *Throw it in the ocean where the sharks are waiting.*

I felt the winds of heaven freeze me. I stood, carrying the figure towards the sea until the water was up to my waist, and I threw it as far as I could. The sea disappeared from my eyes.

My students' paintings survived the saltwater and so did I.

For several years, the dress remains a dress inside my closet until the day I'm ready and I ask my daughter if she will make it into a quilt. And she does. And it covers me, holds me, until I fall asleep.

Throw me in the ocean where the sharks are waiting...

Why I Write

I write to find beauty in places where people think that it could never exist. I write to challenge conventions. More often than not, however, I write to find beauty, especially in people.

Jon Tobias

BORDER CROSSING

Mike Stang

From where I stand, over there, the land on the other side of the dragon bridge, is a land I am yet to see. In fact Japan is a land I am yet to see, but here I stand, not seeing it.

Fine by me, I think, shifting camera equipment to the other hip, *the less I see the sooner I leave.*

I was hired as a freelancer by a startup group, bunch of soft new kids recently collated out of Hawaii University. Typical money-eyed juveniles relying on a best-guess program to fame and daddy's fortune. I thrive off these guys and others like them. Cruising along their flanks like a shark, the smell of another brilliant ad drives me nuts. I'm the support gal with the right package: project research, media base, photos, copy—the staff. I fix what they can't and pull down a decent wage doing it. Oh, I could scam for a ton more. The *lolos* back at the office don't read copy, don't know layout; they do clueless real good, just the way I like them, still, it's the *wahine mokupuni* in me [island woman], that keeps me honest—I guess.

The campaign is as much a dud as the company. They want a photo spread of Japan's least populated northern key for a pitch that makes no sense. The area is known to be a protected archaeological site, lots of local legend and mythological fame. One of the legends, I discovered during my initial investigation, a legend any real estate agent would keep to themselves, is at the northern quarter of the island there exists a border between the realm of the living, and the realm of the dead—who knew? The sector is hidden within an amusement park. Think Country Japanese or Mickey at sixty! USSR is the next island up the chain. Charming. Tell me what does a place like this have to do with selling shaving cream, and what does that have to do with dead people? It's by me, but hey, I didn't care, it all paid the same.

27

My plan is to stay away from the Russians, snap a few shots of indigenous researchers, a bullshit temple or two and be gone. Get back on a plane and be snuggled away in my fourth-floor, one room studio—saddled up and spying on skinny men's penises as they parade down Hilo's public beach— in less than fifteen hours.

Like I said, that was the plan. Well, the plan developed engine trouble over the Pacific and we were diverted to Guam for a three hour lay-over. By the time I arrived in-country my quickie turned over-nightie. Though not much consolation, I figure as long as I don't have to get too close to the food (those noodle bowls they serve with squirming bits of living), and, don't have to touch someone, god forbid, I suppose the money is right enough.

~

The bridge is advertised to look like one of Japan's dragon-gods of old— Ryūjin himself from his crystal palace at the bottom of the sea. Glittered with tide jewels straight out of mythos-histories, the ancient monster is as impatient than ever to reclaim Japan's lost glory for himself. My kind of dragon. Through acrylic eyes painted on the side of the arched wooden expanse, I can feel his exasperation; I must be psychic, right? Ten-thousand years stuck behind history-dust is a whole lot of impatience.

It remains unclear whether or not the "adventure" bragged about in a brochure I hold in my hands, takes me on the ride of my life, or a spin through a mocked-up fantasy village, full of ghost images geared towards the five and under. A closer look at the photoshop pictures reveals the dragon's motif as nothing more than a Carney-bauble to hook you in. Scam, fake, tinsel, I think. Those idiots in Hawaii booked me to a Nihonjin (Japanese) wanna-be Disneyland. If *I* was a dragon hell bent on revenge, I would fire-breathe the lot of them back to the ether; that would be first on a growing list of issues. Ryūjin's breath however, forged from the core of the earth and the strength of the sun compared to my mealy flicker, means the world is in for some serious fury.

It is only a matter of time before Ryūjin goes berserk.

I had no idea where the boys in the office got their intel from, but this backwater ditch hastily refitted to a world heritage site—a famous working scholarly retreat—is anything but.

The facade of the place is weather rotted plywood, twenty feet long and at least as high. Light breezes wobble the framing; a hole cut in the center admits the day trippers. On the side facing out, a mural decays from years of neglect. Historical scenes from Japan's grandeur are lost forever except in the memories of the old ダファー (duffers) who hang out in the corners like they got something to do. Back home we call them nā wīwī (no dicks).

A rush of early morning monks hold their ever-present begging bowels low under narcissistic eyes, as I make my way to a row of turnstiles set to milk yen from the day's crowd. The smell of cooking rises with the mist from vendor's vats: miso soup, sukiyaki, steaming shabu using local meat from mountain goats that tramp this dead-end world. Finger aromas led visitors deeper into the mire, blissfully unaware, they run between attractions with paper bowels and plastic chop sticks. I run looking for a quiet place to gag.

The site is rotten with tourists. Not a religious archeologist to be found. What GPS guided, rock pick carrying earth-nerd would choose to spend a day at their favorite stupa, in the mud up to their necks in search of prehistoric relics the size of a gnat's leg, when invasion is close at hand by groups of sun blocked, designer-sneakered Martians ready to trespass through the dig's grid; little Johnny and bigger Suzzie pulling up elevation stakes to play swords?

A sense of the impossible settles on my otherwise over confident *moke* shoulders. Amusement park, or sacred ground? Kiddy ride, or a tour to the realm of the dead—what's real? Which is it? Besides, who will pay me to find out? I'm in this country to get shots of Scandinavian buddhist blondes (Remember her?), enticing men to take it all off, not go trampling into the mystic. What about Ryūjin? I keep feeling him push me to the dragon bridge. Have to be careful around the likes of him, one puff in anger and I end up in the dead zone—dead.

The signs leading to the bridge are easy to follow. Caricature monks doodled in the margins point to text written in Kana transliteration. They got western cowboys thumbing over at English approximations. In one language or another I'll find it.

According to an exhaustive whiteboard on display inside a makeshift museum run by the state, the earth spat two pitons out of the Sea of Japan some millions of years ago. Rumor has it these isolated pillars of geological gloat were considered sacred land, ruled by deities who created portals on earth where departed souls could enter the hereafter. *So*, I think, *these yahoo's I work for want to advertise dead people enjoying a morning shave*—hmm—a real show-stopper.

Binoculars and stationary telescopes are for rent, bringing you closer to the action. In the living territory, this side of the bridge, blue skies, and warm air run up to a shadow across the land. Pass that perpetual storms, dark and forbidden, obscure the future of anyone who dares to enter. That's exactly where I want to go. This is more like it. Maybe I could make something out of this wasted assignment after all. I count on the dragon, fake or not, to take me there.

Naming places and giving titles to people and things reaches a level of sanctity in the Land of the Rising Sun, to a point that foreigners risk losing body parts for high crimes of mispronunciation, or—beyond all imagination—ridicule. Fortunately, the listicle gives western translations. The pitons are called *The Children's Tears*.

Legend claims a follower of the Buddha by the name of *Mizo* held himself responsible for the safety and deliverance of lost souls, particularly children's. Through no fault of their own, these where the abused and forgotten that wandered the grey existence of afterlife. They worked hard labour under the hands of unholy spirits. The revered monk smuggled these haunted spirits across the dragon bridge beneath his great cape, and set them free in the dead zone where they could put meat on those spiritual bones and eventually enter that special place, Japanese believers call Pure Land.

Mizo is a bodhisattva (Sanskrit, 'a person whose essence is perfect knowledge'), and a damn good one. He is a fierce protector of his children willing to give his life to ensure they come to no harm, but don't take my word for it; the litany is all here, come read it for yourself.

It is impossible to walk anywhere in Japan without stepping on a temple's toes. An addicted, seedy monk greets me as I approach one of the four shrines located on the property. Two hundred pounds of sweating pulse shoves a greedy bowel in my face. Cataract lidded eyes avert mine as I catch his telepathic demand. A pocket full of yen is his religion, the means before hightailing it to the local den. I was astonished at myself giving him coins: couple of coppers mixed in with a few nickeled flower blossoms, and a silver looking thing without a hole—I had no idea. The 'Lama' takes off when a couple of armed Prefectural's appear. They drill me with you-should-know-better look, and go away. I slough into the temple I have just paid a king's ransom to do so.

Turns out the shrine has recently gone through a restoration. Taking up the entire back wall a larger than life, reclining Shakyamuni—made from antiquity's finest fiberglass—bares his message to the world. Something came over me; who knows—a living bit? The eyewash of this place shifts and what is left at the bottom of the pan is for fools, but there is no denying an undercurrent beginning to tap dance on my nerves.

The Buddha's face startles me. A patch of uncoated meshing under the nose where the craftsman left his misguided sense of humor, pisses me off. The disfigurement leaves the 'enlightened one,' looking like Adolf Hitler ascended the throne. I'm not buddhist, my parents are more in the animistic camp, a Polynesian thing, but this obvious level of bigotry turns my stomach as hard as a plate full of sushi.

Jizo, and the kids keep tugging at my craw. I start to focus on a wild-ass idea of taking the dragon out for a spin past those Pitons. I am queer when it comes to the dead, I want to see how they live, maybe take a few shots, sneak around a bit—now there's a story. What I really want is a chance to break into my own fieldwork. Forget about the wage. Open the world up to arcane sides of life, highlight people who believe in the abstract. I want to get hazy, dirty, esoteric and filthy rich. Do a little throne climbing myself. Good riddance to Hilo and its 130+ inches of rainfall per year.

Of course I don't expect zombies, but an ancient religious ritual is not out of the question. To be the first to film it and get it published would mean—_not_ having the time to watch skinny dicks from my suite, high above Tokyo City: a gated community lined with stupa shaped Gingko trees and manservants—_unless_ I want to.

I follow a family group from Australia who seem real in their respect for this otherwise roadside attraction. Unlike the rash Americans: crazed elephants stomping ahead of their tails made of sugar diets and screaming kids about to piss their pants.

The trail to the bridge is thankfully off the beaten path and rugged enough to discourage the less inclined. Even the Aussies split up and allow the more focused to study the expanse on their own. I hang around in the background trying to keep my eyes off the _haoles,_ those _down-under_ men sporting muscular thighs in safari shorts. Instead I notice a control box that hangs on one the bridge's railings. Light, steady rain promises I will have the place to myself. Japanese mist moves in tight over the ground, a romantic mystique I can do without.

Two _Sanpais_ (elders), in traditional high and dry _Minos_ (rain gear of straw), stand close enough to the gate to be guardians. From the looks of them I'd say they are local farts with everything to say about every little thing. As I approach, they don't speak to me rather about me, to each other. It seems I need their permission to access the dragon bridge and decide diplomatic politeness is best.

White speckled hands erupt in front of my face as the old crows cry out in indignant terror. I bow and scrap my way to less than a foot from the bridge. At first I think they are hitting on me for an unseen yen-to-pocket transfer, but the issue was the camera around my neck. Not allowed. Hands turn to wagging fingers _e kū_ they shout in flawless Hawaiian (stop), 'a'ohe ki'i kamepiula (no camera). I'm impressed. Maybe it's my thicker than blood haule'a lauoho lauwili (crazy natural hair), that gives me away.

They keep wailing and pointing at the camera between my breasts. Then I get it, these dogs realize I'm a woman alone. A woman without a man who wants to take the dragon ride around the village, see the sights, take forbidden pictures. Their expressions say it all. I'm dealing with two leftovers from a dynastic era when to be a woman was to be a slave. Born into servitude at any level of society: crippled feet, stretched neck, the look of fugly beauty for your husband's eyes ... slave.

No one else is around, I can't see two feet in front of me, I'm alone with two men who are about to take advantage of a situation. Mentally I imagine drawing my *ka pahi kaua hanohano* (Hawaiian honor sword), and separating their heads from their necks. Ryūjin is ready just below the surface, pushing against the limits of my reality. Leathery wings gear up enormous strength.

Nobody is going to keep me from my dragon, especially these two dirt bags. I swing the camera's case with all my might and wipe out their shins down towards their ridiculously raised *getas*—whoever invented stilted sandals is a sadist. At the same time I make the jump onto the bridge and clutch the panel solid in my hands. The earth beneath me opens up, I press the green button hoping it means go—it does. An ancient monster releases into modern day; I push the orange button hoping that means go faster—yes!

Ryūjin detonates to life in front of me. Everything I am shifts to a different reality. The dragon-god waits only for a second for me to climb on his shoulders. Everything else I am will have to wait until after.

If there is an after.

The *Sanpais* grow small as the dragon rises into the mist laced sky. *Does everything in this country come with a cloud?* The one with the longest *Fu Manchu* is already talking into his smart phone; Shakyamuni himself if I had to guess. The other is ransacking my case which holds credentials and passport. No turning back now; this is for keeps.

The dragon and I time-warp and are gone.

Ryūjin surrounds me with his majestic body. Unflinchingly, we ride the winds as a team in search of Jizo's legend. We own the skies like we own each other. On fabled wings I ride his scaly back holding tight to noble horns. Above the clouds we soar to snow-capped piton's peaks and circle their magnificent summits.

I'm free and reckless as we screech through the day's light, and leave warm air in our vapor's trail. I'm Indiana Jones racing to the Holy Grail, with full intentions to take what I came for and escape to a life of pleasure. This is my turn. I deserve it.

At the speed of light we enter the realm of the dead. Ryūjin is prepared for this, I'm not. I scream and dig my nails raw into his scales. Panic consumes me. I want to go back to the living land. This is too much unknown for a simple Hawaiian girl trying to make a buck, but my dragon ignores me. There will be no turning back.

The air is thick and constantly moves in on itself; the wind locomotive. We land on a mesa surrounded by low swamp of murky boil. I feel the heat immediately and something else, something alive is pulling me under the surface. I hear it, him—them—the beat of millions. Amidst impassioned pleas to Jizo, Shakyamuni, my own Kahōʻaliʻi and anybody else with any say to my safety, Ryūjin flexes one of his wings and sends me aerial through the brown air headlong into the swamp.

Shock takes hold of my body but is no match for the anger I have for the dragon. My feet trap in roily silt. This is the end tricked by a monster. He doesn't need me, I'm not part of Ryūjin's two-faced scheme. Better to kill me quick and get on with it. I am the fool he waited on to set him free— orange button. Just thinking of how I thought everyone else were fools makes me shake. I meet my fate hapless, seething with revenge.

The underbelly begins to clear. I find I'm able to breathe. Maybe I won't die today. The rhythm I heard on the surface is now a deep, vibrating chant that shakes my bones. I hear them all, thousands of them. Collected spirits guided by steadfast ropes of healing energy. Jizo is still at it, bound by his compassion for sentient beings. The legends are true, I see for myself what any devotee would give everything to witness.

There is a presence behind me; huge and heavy—overpowering. When I turn, three stories of giant stands over me. Naked, unfortunately just to the waist, he is the figure of the beast. The muscular development is grotesque to a degree it's hard for me to tell whether it flesh or armor. A green patina gives me the impression he's mechanical. An AI? No, no way, I shake my head and look again. His head is shaven except for a top knot of hair tightly woven like a bee's hive from which fat ribbons of great length, pure silk, banner down to his feet. Facial features are advanced beyond anything human, and yet I can clearly see he has the face of a Samurai: cold, fierce, intelligent. His eyes reflect every bit of ten thousand years committed to this world. Over his right shoulder lays the great cape he uses to hide the children, protecting them while crossing realms.

There is no question Bodhisattva Jizo stands before me.

Here I am, some trick photographer looking for a get rich scheme so I can spend it on a life of greed. What wouldn't I do to get ahead of everybody else? Look at me now, ready to exploit the children to serve my own advantage; a chance of a lifetime, the pot of gold. Snatch the souls of the innocent to photoactive cells, capture the great Jizo himself, the working deity, to nothing but a field shot.

The sound of helicopter blades fill my ears. Of course they were coming, I wouldn't be allowed to flee. Where's kēlā diakona hōʻailona—that fucking dragon when I need him the most? I figure by now most of Tokyo has burned to the ground . Hopelessly I fall on my knees head bowed. The camera drops from my grip lost to the bottom. In defeat I prepare myself for the worst—Jizo's judgement.

The giant had me in his sights. I freeze as he reaches out his hands, palms up, to touch my face. The last thing I remember is how the mythological hero opens his mouth wide enough to swallow the earth. There's intense, a warm glow, then nothing at all.

❦

The darkness is soft, inviting, a cocoon of comfort and safety. I want to stay in there forever, left alone to sleep. There's a bed under me. I'm astonished when I open my eyes and realize the bed is my own. I'm home, back in the studio overlooking Hilo beach. What the ... ?

Getting up is a hard check on reality, my body provides the bullet list: dislocated shoulder, bone strain, muscle sprains, cuts and bruises; blisters everywhere. There's enough goo and gauze on me I look like mortal remains. Then there's the sound of footsteps coming from the kitchen. *Someone's in my house.* I turn my head too quickly and am rewarded with shooting star pains. It's one of the lolos from the office, Anakoni I think. He carries a tray with tea glasses, a plate of food and a stupid grin.

I watch all this from the ceiling, out of body, not sure if I'm dead or alive. One moment I was flying with a dragon-god headed into ... Oh shit: the assignment! The park, the monks; bridge, dragon, pitons, the memories! Did it really happen? Ryūjin! If I ever get my hands on him again I'll send that lizard back to his watery grave.

I remember Jizo and the children. My camera?

Anakoni, besides being parent spoiled, stuck up and oblivious, is kind of cute in a Pacific-Rim sort of way. The slender body reminds me of the male beach parade. I steal a look over at the telescope perched in front of the windows then steal one at the bulge in his pants. The faux executive babbles about how great and brave and stunning I am to have turned his ad idea into a multi-leveled, millions of dollars success. He shows me a video of a Japanese craftsman, leaning off a scaffold, fixing the upper lip of a reclining Shakyamuni. I'm not listening when Anakoni explains how I tracked the creep down and made him fix his little joke. I drink my tea and nod; I don't remember anything.

There are other videos, lots of them. My soon to be boy-toy shows them to me non- stop: two sanpais were arrested over sexual assault charges from women tourists, a crew had to restore a Japanese idyllic, arched bridge after seismic activity blew it off its foundation, another crew replaced the park's plywood facade; a suspicious fire at the offices of historical education in downtown Tokyo is under control after an eight hour battle, and finally a global broadcast from Moscow, standing down a previous broadcast that declared a nuclear response to Japan's invasion of Soviet air space over their southern-most islands. The results reported by the USSR, after an

34

investigation into the incident, described unexplained wings the size of an aircraft carrier and the body of a bird with an extremely long tail. Definitely not missiles.

Thankful there are no mentions of a rider, I turn the recorder off.

In the middle of all the fascinating news, Anakoni stops and asks me if I learned anything about the living-dead realms. From his body language, which to me has all the implications of getting on his knees to thank me again—properly, he doesn't believe in any of it.

I see there's no write up about bodhisattvas or children. No photos, videos, nothing. My mind traces the last moments in Japan, right after Jizo opened his mouth, and the warmth fell over me. What happened after that I really don ... wait a minute, the blanket, yes I'm sure of it. Jizo threw the blanket over me like he does with his children to protect them as they cross the bridge. He must've crossed me back over to the living side; get me out of where I didn't belong.

It makes sense. The last thing a bodhisattva needs is a media curse cause by a naive idiot who doesn't know shit about anything, besides, from the look of me—thanks to jerk-off Ryūjin—I feel Jizo had my safety in mind.

I lost the most important story of my life that day; sure enough I'm on Japan's no fly list, but something better happened out there. A buddhist saint manhandled me to safety. In doing so Jizo shared his compassion like a secret note slipped into my pocket to read when I got home. He's my new man-god hero, I'll never forget that chiseled chest or the sight of those children.

Anakoni, bless his inflamed libido, pulls out the big guns: ten million from film rights, another 2.8 to publish the book; royalties forever. He says 2.5 percent of that is mine plus the world wants to know who I am and when would I be free to set up a meeting? I'll hold off telling him he's confused. 100 percent of the money is mine, and I'll write him a check to cover any losses for *not* delivering a backdrop for his stupid can of shaving cream. His lips reach for mine, but I'm already snuggled away in my cocoon.

In the morning I sit at the telescope netting early male walkers, when they think no one is watching and take a piss behind the dunes. Coffee and a shocking cigarette are my only distractions. It will take a couple of days for the shock to wear off, but Anakoni can try again whenever he wants, I'm not going anywhere. Tokyo is the glimmer pot and that's all well and good, but the Big Island is my 'oko'a and it's about time I got into it.

A month has passed since my return and I am still picking hairs out of my poi. Yesterday a poster hanging at my favorite Starbucks informed me Rev. Ichido Uchida, one of Japans leading authorities on buddhism, was giving a lecture at the university. I called Anakoni to tell him to get over it and pick me up at eight. The hall was tiny so we had great seats. After the session a distinguished looking gentleman approached us and asked if I would accompany him backstage to meet the monk. I was thrilled in the way someone is thrilled to pick up a hot pan. Uchida met us at his door and stated he only wanted to talk to me. Not missing a beat, the gentleman walked Anakoni over to the saki bar. It seemed to me the Reverend was on edge and in a hurry to get this over with. I asked if something was wrong, and he told me he wasn't accustomed to dealing with deities and took a crumbled piece of paper from his pocket. I didn't know what to say as he handed me the scrap.

"He has your camera."

*It's none of their business you have to learn to write. Let them think
you were born that way.*

Ernest Hemingway

FLAMING FIELDS

Laura Elizabeth

I'll tell you a secret. The boy with hair like flaming fields loves me. Red curls lick my fingers as we kiss for hours in his tree house after school. Goats swish the rain-glossed blackberry leaves, tasting the world like we are.

He stands outside the bulletproof glass at my last class till I'm free. He hot-wires Bertha, his baby blue Bel Air, to get her started. The boys in Corvettes laugh, but respect his matter-of-fact shoulders, the safety pin in his cheek. He winks like Santa, says punk is just a fashion. He rescues the boy in the wheelchair when others throw him in the dumpster.

He comes to the door to meet my mother in his black leather jacket, with no shirt underneath. When she's not looking, he flashes my name in delicate scabs over his heart. There's always a note in our pockets, just received or about to be given. He draws us popping freckled puffballs in the forest, with captions for what we talk about: materialism or mountain light. He draws a heart bubble around us so we do this forever, on paper at least.

"I love you. Someday I will marry you," he carves on a branch I keep under my bed. He wants to build a cabin, a baby of pure love. I'd rather hike the world first, write the story to stop all wars. At least go to college. Thirty's a good age, not sixteen.

He lives in a trailer, where a skylight holds one piece of sky. It's enough. When it rains, his family opens the windows to let the storm inside. They touch as they pass in the hall that holds them tight. They listen to what I love: the Three Sisters mountains, how they hold me like a family.

Our clothing is a country we take time to explore. The Who sings "Love, Reign O'er Me" over and over, as violet lightning strikes the land. His thumbs play the song inside me, and I glisten like wet moss on the oaks outside. We could go all the way like everyone. But we'd miss the journey from mouth to shoulder blade, thigh hair to navel fuzz, what we think to what we feel. Like one piece of sky, it's enough.

When my parents assume and ground me, he sews me a beaded leather pouch for protection. Inside are fir needles, quartz from our walks, a tiny pink ring from Woolworth's. He bikes miles uphill to kiss me goodnight through my bedroom window screen. Every night for months, our kisses taste of metal, and his notes are soaked with tears instead of Old Spice.

Twenty years later, I find the power pouch, filled with forests and the sparkling crystals of our bodies. The dime store ring, the carved branch that says it straight. We're adults now. Do men still nick our names in skin, take time to stoke the fire? Do they listen to what we love, use their power to protect our hearts? If they no longer say it straight, that is love lost. I watch for violet lightning. Love, Reign O'er Me.

Then, the world beckoned...

Why I Am An Editor.

In addition to their stories, the five authors we're showcasing include their self-perception of why they write, each with motives unique to themselves. It occurred to me that having asked them to confess, I should do the same. Why am I an editor?

Here goes:

I was the skinny kid with glasses who held the jacket when somebody with more balls than me had had enough and was going to punch somebody's lights out in the playground after school. I observed the passions—sometimes volatile passions—of life's real participants, from the safety of the sidelines.

I lived my adventures for the longest time vicariously, a type b, lower case, ten-point font, in a world intimidated by type A's, bold, maybe even italicized and underlined, Franklin Gothic Heavy.

Then, the world beckoned, and I dabbled in high risk, exposing first myself and eventually my family to unconscionable danger (such as paying a smuggler to get us across the Straights of Malacca in a sampan at two in the morning after the gunboats passed).

One day while shaving I saw the first lines penciling across my forehead, and then I knew it; I wasn't holding somebody else's jacket anymore, and somewhere along the line I stopped living my life like a turtle crossing a highway.

Though retelling my (mis)adventures can hold anybody's attention for a half an hour at a dinner party, I know the best stories are the ones that take place under the skin.

Tell me a story about climbing Mount Everest, and I am already bored. I know what it's all about. You climb. There is risk. You almost die. You have an epiphany. You come down off the mountain. You write a book about it.

BUT...tell me how you screwed up your marriage(s). Tell me what went wrong, what *you* did wrong. Tell me how your youngest daughter ended up in prison, and why it should be you in her place. Tell me of the insurrections that you yourself led with every relationship that ever meant anything to you, who you wanted to murder, and why. Who wanted to murder you, and why. Tell me of sabotage and heresy and destruction and betrayal and mutiny, redemption and infinite "second" chances and of pain and of pleasure and fury, and the *joy* you carved out for yourself in spite of it all. Tell me these things, and you have my attention, and I will hold your jacket after school in the playground. Old habits die hard.

I became an editor because *you* have a story, yet to be told.

I'm listening.

Thornton Sully
Editor-in-Chief
A Word with You Press

The funny thing about working with Thorn is that I can't exactly say what he does that helps me. I usually start out not agreeing with his suggestions, only to end up following them. Maybe it's the very act of resisting his ideas that serves as an exercise in clarification. After all, more times than not, this exercise leads me to see the wisdom of his direction. Perhaps it's Thorn practical wisdom on the art and craft of writing. I'm still not sure. All I know is I've become a better writer since working with Thorn.

– Mark Cohen, author
Listening to the Echo

Mike Stang
Why I Write

I am a lone wolf. I self-instruct, and take to the high trails less traveled.

By these words I mean to say I am no better than another brother or sister with pen in hand and a far cry from the masters. Thousands of other writers make me drool they are so good. No, what happens is I write alone: Me, my muse and I, and she, the silent stimulus; a medicine to take and feel better in retrospect.

A warm, sincere thank-you to the other writers who have extended their kindness and time to help me along. Diane Cresswell, Sara Crysl Akhtar, Thornton Sully, Steve Sellers and Jeff Swift. How lucky can a writer get?

In reference to published work, I would not be published if it was not for Thornton Sully and the towers at *A Word with You Press*. Other sites include Molotov Cocktail, *molotovcocktail.com* and Medium, *medium.com*.

It is difficult to say whether I will come down off the mountain. I do not know. Writing is my bridge to forever land. I am having too much fun.

Mike lives near the west coast of the United States of America, in California under the same roof as his lovely wife of forty years, Betty, a dog of nine years, Pumpkin, and various cats of undetermined rotation. You are invited to contact him at *whitedragon421gmail.com*.

*Don't bend; don't water it down; don't try to make it logical; don't edit
your own soul according to the fashion.
Rather, follow your most intense obsessions mercilessly.*

— Franz Kafka

Dancing House (Tančící dům): bending reality in the city of Kafka

MEMORIES

Jon Tobias

The dim, yellow light hums like a wall of fluorescent lights. Emerson swears it even ripples like rain on lake water but being completely engulfed in it, there is no way to know if that is true or not. He has the disorienting sensation of being under water with no sight of surface or floor.

"If you could go back to any place in your life where would you go?" The voice, coming from nowhere and everywhere, is a soft child-like whine. It is as if the owner's vocal chords are made up of many doors creaking open in quiet rooms.

"What? Where am I?"

"Anywhere, any-when you want?"

"Am I dreaming?"

Emerson last remembers microwaving a lunch plate in his lonely apartment. As he went to take it out his chest began to hurt. He remembers falling and yelling *help*. He remembers his old hands grasping his chest before collapsing to the kitchen floor.

"You have to choose," the light whines.

"Choose what?"

"A place. A time in your life."

Emerson is suddenly aware of his heart, which feels heavy and is pumping so hard that he feels it pounding against his back.

"There, there was an apartment. I lived in it with this girl when I was younger---"

Emerson stands in the kitchen of a two-bedroom apartment he lived in as a young man. An empty dish sits on the stove, but he can still smell the melted butter, and garlic, and vegetables that were once inside. He walks out of the kitchen a little to where the tile meets the living room carpet. Emerson sees Nicole sitting on the couch smiling and staring at her phone.

The plates from the dinner he made them both are still sitting on the coffee table. She has no makeup on, and the freckles across the bridge of her nose are illuminated by the phone light. Emerson loved it when she didn't wear makeup because the freckles stood out. He always thought they made her that much more beautiful.

How did I fuck us up so badly, Emerson says to himself.

The bathroom door swings open, and Emerson watches his young self rush through the hallway towards the front door.

"I'm late."

"Wait." Nicole says, and starts towards him, but he doesn't hear. Emerson shuts the door before she can reach him or say anything else. The look on her face is that of child who thinks she has been forgotten. She probably knows he was just in a rush to work, but Emerson understands what it feels like to be looked over. In that moment he wishes he had stopped long enough to kiss her goodbye. If not that then at least long enough to actually say goodbye. They had only just started dating at this point but were already living together because he was renting a room in her apartment. The renting came first, then late nights watching shows together, then walks to get sushi in the neighborhood, then the realization that love moved in when neither was looking and had its hands on both of their shoulders.

Nicole picks up the dishes from the coffee table and sets them down in the sink before heading towards the bedroom. Emerson follows her but stops at the doorway, allowing her to shut the door in his face. Though she cannot see him, the feeling is the same as if she could.

Emerson realizes as soon as she shut the door that for all the things he thought ended their relationship there could have been countless things he didn't even know about. Allowing someone to become part of the background, a piece of furniture, a passing thought. How many little things had he missed? How many goodbyes and goodnights went unsaid? Emerson decides he must be in Hell.

Why did he want to come back to this exact point anyway? Emerson walks back into the kitchen and stares at the swirling grease in the baking dish. Before realizing what he is doing Emerson picks up the dish and slams it back down on the stove top. The sound is anxious and never ending like coming home drunk and going to pull a plate out of a cupboard to microwave leftovers, but instead of just taking one plate, all the plates come crashing down. The next sound is the metal clicking of a lock followed by the creak of her old bed as Nicole climbs back into it.

Emerson's head begins to hurt right behind his eyes. Soft, yet overwhelming, light fills his vision.

"You shouldn't do that," the voice says.

"Am I a ghost?"

"You're energy."

"How was I able to do that?"

"You still exist, but you shouldn't change things."

Before Emerson can ask why, he feels his memories of then next morning splitting into two for a moment before coming back together and being a single memory where the glass broke.

"Where am I?"

"You're everywhere and everywhen."

"How am I here."

"Your energy left your body and you came here."

"Are you an angel?"

"I just facilitate your movement through time."

"Send me back to—"

Emerson is back in the apartment. He watches himself come home from his nightshift and go into the kitchen for a beer to help him nap. The dish is still shattered.

Young Emerson texts Nicole, "Morning. Everything okay. There's glass all over the kitchen."

He cleans up the mess, slicing his finger open as he picks up rogue shards he finds on the counter top. Nicole does not respond, but he knows she is terrible at responding to texts as well as answering her phone.

That night, the two of them sit on the couch, share a California burrito and watch *Blazing Saddles*.

"Maybe it broke because it was too hot and you didn't put it in the sink," she says before taking a big bite of her half of the burrito.

"I thought for a second you were mad at me."

"Do you honestly think I would do that? I might key your car or ignore you for a week."

"So, it might have been you."

They both laugh.

"I'm sorry I didn't say goodbye last night."

"You were in a rush to work."

"I'm still sorry."

"Maybe we have a ghost," she says.

"That's probably what it was. That makes way more sense."

"I didn't do it."

"I know. I'm sorry for asking. We definitely have a ghost."

"You hear that, Ghost! We know you're here, so stop breaking our shit. We're poor college kids." She laughs again, and Emerson smiles at her.

Emerson watches himself stare at her, and both Emersons smile the same stupid, lovestruck smile.

"I'm going to bed," Nicole says.

"You don't want to finish the movie?"

"I'm tired."

"Goodnight this time." He laughs a little at the joke.

This time, instead of allowing Nicole to shut the door in his face, Emerson follows her into the bedroom, leaving his dumb, young self to finish his burrito half and the rest of the movie.

Emerson remembers wishing she would stay. He remembers wishing he hadn't asked if she broke the dish. He decides he can do something about it this time.

After Nicole sets her phone down by the side of her bed and closes her eyes, Emerson lightly scratches at the far wall. Like a rough fingertip on a chalkboard, he drags his finger along the wall in one solid, smooth motion. With his one finger still pressed firmly, he walks the perimeter of the room until he gets to the wall by the bed, then very gently rolls a pen off the nearby nightstand so the sound of the rolling is obvious and deliberate.

Nicole hears every sound. Emerson knows because he watches her eyes trace the direction of the sound. As soon as the pen hits the floor, she shouts, "Em!"

The room goes white. This time there are little spots of red floating about like the spots a person sees after rubbing his or her eyes too hard.

"I told you."

Emerson ignores the voice and waits to feel the memories of his life change. Instead of going to bed alone, Nicole called him into the room. She thought there really had been a ghost. He tried to convince her the apartment was old, and it was all a coincidence, but she asked him to sleep with her anyway. He did. He didn't believe the ghost was real, but from then on it was their inside joke, and part of the story he told people about how they started to fall for one another.

"Why can't I?"

"Your mind will break into a million pieces. You'll go crazy." The sound that follows could be described as trying to start up a truck under water. Emerson decides it is laughter.

"Why do you let me go back then."

"So you have something to do for the rest of time. You can always stay here forever." The light flickers sporadically.

Before Emerson can say anything else, he finds himself once again in the apartment. Neither he nor Nicole is home, but he notices a vase full of sunflowers on the coffee table, and two picture frames with photos of the two of them. Like finding trinkets in a storage container that is finally being cleaned out, little moments come back to him as if he had simply forgotten them and needed a reminder.

Emerson takes one flower out of the vase and lays it down on the table. In his head it is something that won't change anything too much with the exception that they will believe they really have a ghost. It is something to make their lives more exciting, as well as give something for Emerson to hold on to for the rest of forever.

The room disappears again.

Emerson remembers Nicole saying that the ghost must be jealous because it can't get her flowers like Emerson can. He remembers joking that he has competition now.

There red in the light has now stretched out into thin jagged lines like many veins pulled out of giant bloodshot eyes.

The voice inside the light says nothing. In the silence, Emerson remembers an entire life with Nicole. He doesn't remember in real time. He remembers the way he would had he lived it, and everything that happened, happened long ago. He has chunks of memory, pieces of broken glass when looked into hold only slivers of moments. Some of them are blurred. Some are clear and perfect like the one of their wedding day.

"None of it is real," the voice finally speaks up.

"I don't know if it is, but it feels real."

"It isn't."

"Is this Hell?"

"It is a lot of things. When would you like to go?"

Emerson isn't sent back anywhere. Instead, he considers the triviality of memory. A person can remember anything he or she wants to, but it is only as good as watching television or reading a book. No matter how hard anyone tries, it will never be possible to recall actual feeling. The skin cannot re-sense lips on a cheek or the soft pressure of another person's back when holding them at night. Perfume on an empty pillow can never be re-smelled. A voice cannot be heard without its speaker. Emerson only has the stories he tells himself about a life he thinks is his. That can't kiss him back or tell him it loves him in a voice that isn't his own.

"Changing things won't change anything. Not the way I want them to."

"Clear!"

The room turns bright white. Emerson has the sensation of cold on his chest. He feels the light.

"Where would you like me to send you?"

"Clear!" Emerson starts to make out shapes behind the light. He feels is lungs, his real lungs, being filled with air. He can almost taste it.

As Emerson's eyes slowly open, as he comes back into his own body, everything that he changed about his life slowly starts to disappear. Without thinking, he yells, "I'm not going back!"

The world goes black.

He has the same sensation of floating, of drowning, but the light is gone. So is the voice. His lifetime with Nicole stills feels as real as it did all the way up to his own death which wasn't alone in an apartment heating up a lunch plate. Here in the blackness, she never dumped him. He never had to not get over her. He never died alone. No, she was there at the side of his bed with eyes like broken sea glass and freckles like a wall of bullets fired and then suspended at a distance.

Yellow dots start to form in the blackness like needles piercing a sheet. They begin to widen. Through one large hole, Emerson hears, "Where would you like to go."

"Nowhere," he says.

As quickly as the holes appeared, they seal themselves leaving Emerson alone in a pitch black nothing.

Romanticize everything.

Jon Tobias

RATED TEXAN

When Gary Clark bellied up to the bar, we were the ones ending up drunk. Gary was a cowboy in every sense of the term, could straddle a rodeo bull and took no bull. He helped energize our website for the years he was with us, all the while knowing that cancer could lay him out at the time of its choosing, which it did—way too soon. What follows is his contest entry we ran on our site—one of more than fifty since we were founded in 2009. Typically, we offer a prompt to enter, and a different but related prompt for those who make the finals. The initial prompt was "I swear, it's not too late." The prompt for finalists was "but by then, it was too late."

We miss you, Cowboy.

WILLIAM JOSEPH CLARK
Gary Clark

...five hours of running the timer at a barrel racing, watching, mentally undressing, and listening to the cowgirls pant and grunt. Their tight butts slapping against hard saddles, they whipped their horses into lather, and raced toward the finish line. I'd already loosened my belt to relieve some of the expanding pressure down there in my Wranglers. I'd even pulled my shirttail out to cover Spike's growing salute to their beauty and skill and tight butts.

Driving home, I promised Spike a night he'd never forget. "Forget about the buckle bunnies from all those other rodeos," I told him, sliding my hand up my right thigh. "Tonight it's all about you, big boy," and I gave him a slow, gentle rub on his bald head. We both slipped into a silent, hopeful dream of things to come when we got home. It was one of those drives home that you walk into your house, look back at the truck and wonder, "How the fuck did I get here?"

Then, from down the hall, we heard the soft crackling of plastic. I jerked my face toward the sound and there she stood, leaning against the doorframe to our bedroom. Wrapped tightly from head to toes in one tight layer of saran wrap, she'd tied a tiny pink bow down there so it barely covered ground zero. Spike struggled to free himself, and I fought hard to hold back the easy line; "Leftovers again?" I knew that comment would cost me and Spike the night of nights, the revenge of the 'nads, and the chance to mentally have our way with each and every one of those barrel racers that taunted and teased us with their easy-on-the-eyes bodies.

I girded my loins, slowly unwrapped her, threw her on the bed and suffered through the obligatory twenty seconds of foreplay. Then I reached down and unleashed Spike. He slapped against my belly, stood proud, growled and sniffed the air. Suddenly, like a Cadillac bursting into a doghouse, he ducked his head and took the plunge.

Spike drove like a lunatic, snarling and penetrating until he hit the bottom of the depths of her lust. She screamed and clawed at my back. I sucked in a deep breath and slammed my chin into my chest. My spine tingled. My heart stopped. My brain was consumed in the swelling orgasm.

In one quick move, she shifted and flipped me on my back, mounted me like a maverick and rode me like a Harley. In the throes of my wildest passion, she popped a wheelie causing me to throw myself from side to side, ripping cotton out of the mattress, hurling pillows across the room and slapping the lamp off the bedside table. I gasped for air like an escaped guppy lying on the tabletop, doubled up my fist and banged on the top of her head trying to break her toothy grip on my ear.

She hit the throttle again leaving me breathless and semi-conscious. I babbled nonsensical phrases, spoke in tongues, and swallowed my tonsils. Then I felt it. My eyes grew as big as saucers. My toes curled back and touched my heels. Unconsciously, I panted those helpless, dying, squeaking noises of a fat mouse caught between the teeth of a barn cat. I was one second away from diving off the cliff and floating down into an earth-shattering, orgasmic oblivion.

She leaned and whispered into the mangled flesh that was once my ear; "The test strip showed I'm at my peak fertility today."

I screamed like a little girl. Squealed like the locked brakes of a speeding freight train, shattering the half-empty glass of water on her bedside table. Sparks flew and hair singed. My brain exploded. I shifted my butt into reverse and struggled to back Spike out of her evil quiver.

"Get the hell outta there, Spike," I yelled. "It's a setup! Get out, quick! I swear it's not too late."

But it was too late. In a once in a lifetime, sky-splitting, teeth grinding, ugly-faced orgasm, three hundred million tadpoles exploded from my loins and raced toward the promised land.

Drained, dehydrated, and deflated, Spike collapsed like a beached jellyfish lying on top of a bearded clam. I lay in a sweaty puddle of utter exhaustion and defeat, writhing without purpose, gasping for air, and praying for a crop failure.

I laid my head against her chest and from deep down inside her body, I heard the small voice of a lone sperm decked out in cowboy hat and spurs. "Hi, I'm Billy Joe Clark," he said, grinning big at the waiting ovum.

She giggled, winked, pulled her ponytail to the side, and invited him in.

I always start writing with a clean piece of paper and a dirty mind.

Patrick Dennis

Laura Elizabeth

...wandered the forests as a girl, penning poems the trees sang. She tries to translate the stories that live in the world already, if only we listen. She considers herself more of a poet than a narrative writer, but she's trying her hand at stories and essays. "I'm grateful to *A Word with You Press* and the whole community of writers for the kick in the pants to sit in the chair."

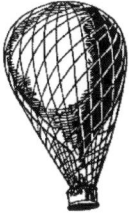

LOVER'S CROSS

Laura Elizabeth

I'd always had a crush on Jesus. When I was younger, my parents dragged me through Europe's cathedrals. They were cruel centerfolds for Jesus, sprawling on wooden crucifixes in a loincloth. He was handsome, sad and kind, like the love I'd always wanted. I wanted to save the Savior from his cross. I'd wipe his wooden tears, wrap him in my arms like Mary. Maybe he'd kiss me. I needed to confess, but I didn't know French.

So when His likeness walked into biology class that sun-sexed college summer, I knew. His Levi's were fashionably tattered. His feet were bare. The port wine stain on his chin made him my Chosen One in a litter of kittens. I decided he was put here on Earth to show me how to love.

On the class field trip to measure the blue purity of Crater Lake, we shared a tent. As the moon rose, he sang me to sleep instead of groping me goodnight. He shook his holy ringlets over me, breathed in his smooth, loose voice, "Dream of blue water." That's when I knew. When others loved me for my body, I felt a rush of relief when he loved me for my soul. He twirled my braids, looked deep inside, asked what mattered. It made me want his body.

He wanted to be an opera singer, but his fallback career plan was respectable in our town: pot dealer. His voice teacher told him to lay off the wacky tobacky, if only to hit high tenor. When he sang "O Holy Night," a forgotten side door in my heart creaked open. I was three again, all blind trust as my father sang his bedtime songs in tenor.

When this man said, "Let's go upstairs and cry about our childhoods," we'd climb the ladder to his attic bedroom, close the trap door, and love on our own time. We'd kiss away salt tears and share our stories in holy communion. His father was a coal miner, came home every hard day to carry his wife to the bathroom, who had MS. As a child he'd shared a bed with his grandma, back to back, to keep her warm. He missed those times.

He seemed handsome, sad and kind, like Jesus. He played Lord Krishna at the hippie fair, spray-painting his body blue and leading his people to peace with a wooden flute. For our nightly sacrament, he always lit the incense. Then he opened my soul with his sacred scepter, exposing my pink, pulsing heart to universal love. I tried to make his imperfections glorious, like God was saying, "Behold. This is how you love a mortal."

I marveled at two hairs sprouting from his skinny left shoulder as he moved above me. I adored the little pink hippie hat he wore to keep his bald spot warm, his feminine scent of patchouli. Above the bed, his yellow button-downs spied on us from a makeshift clothesline. I loved those shirts, even though he looked terrible in yellow. They were so full of him, even when he was gone. When he polished his pirate boots with a black Sharpee to dress up for a party, I knew again.

He was a recovering Baptist, so we rewrote Adam and Eve with our bodies. If we loved each other enough, it wasn't a sin, and we could even save the world with it. Crosby, Stills & Nash's first album was our scripture. And God said: *They are one person, They are two alone, They are three together, They are for each other.*

In our twenties, it seemed possible to make love, to manufacture it, in the soul through the body. Polite courting paled in comparison to the honest flood of emotions freed through our bodies' gates. He fed me Eve's apples gleaned from trees around town, showed me how to shimmy naked in moonlight. He built a backyard sweat lodge of blankets and river sticks, fanned away his flock's fears with holy sage.

The day the world became a matriarchy, I moved in. I always bowled either gutters or strikes, but that day I was on a roll of love. I said if I won, the Earth's axis would flip and women would rule. We bowled for peace on Earth, and when I won, he happily obliged. He said he'd wanted that all along.

It seemed true. He always opened with, "I want to hold you," and later, "I want to please you." Even his refrigerator magnets were politically correct: "Give Peace and Chance" and "Give Pigs a Chance." He called his chickens his ladies, fought for their freedom from the cranky rooster. He only ate their eggs, and filled the fridge with tofu. He seemed like a good bet after the usual bevy of patriarchs.

For a few months, we lived in bliss in the tumbledown tofu house. One day, he pulled his prize from behind the bed. The aging violin had his thin shoulders and tear-jerking tenor. His grandpa owned a music store in coal country. He said it was a Stradivarius, that we'd sell it and travel the world.

I secretly questioned this retirement policy, since the violin was already baking to a crisp in the attic. But I dreamed of building a cabin of pure love, dyeing his boxer shorts green with forest moss. Bearing his skinny, big-footed son, who would also be Jesus.

All those dreams died the night he threw the 20-pound dartboard at my head. Something about my male friends, even though he whispered to women each night on the phone while I experimented with the moss to get his boxers right.

Maybe he was mad he couldn't reach high tenor with wacky tobacky, and switched to whiskey. Or maybe the Earth's axis had simply flipped back to the patriarchy. Somewhere, a cosmic gutter ball had been rolled.

Without the little pink hat, the veins stood out on his head like my father's. The dartboard narrowly missed my head, and tore a hole in the wall. Then he overturned a table and broke the vase of skunky irises I'd gathered for him. They lay there, shaking with dew, like the ones I used to bring my mother to coax her smile. I curled into a ball, felt five again. "What about the flowers?" was all I could stutter.

The night before, I'd dreamed of a giant black and yellow insect on that same wall. Its stripes flashed a warning. I'd pushed it aside, since I'd save the world if I turned the other cheek. My mother said so. But somehow, I managed to duck just in time. Somehow, after offering my sacred chalice to light his dark matter, there was still a tiny piece of me that was mine.

Maybe a big piece, considering how fast I yanked my furniture out while he slept off the patriarchy. As I dragged my heavy cherry cabinet out all by myself, it was my heart that left gouges on the floor, holding onto the dream of his thighs for dear life.

For months afterward, I had the strange sensation that one last piece of me still hovered like a ghost in the attic, exactly where his left shoulder would have been. In the corner of my eye, those two hairs danced at the edge of the frame. I buried poems in earth at the cemetery, trying to put the dream of love to rest. I dreamed he nailed me to the cross.

I fantasized about buying bullets at the hardware store. I'd also buy the CSN cassette, placing one bullet in each hole. Then I'd drop the cassette in the mailbox of the tofu house. That'd show him he'd shot our songs to death and taught me it's wrong to love. *Love isn't lying, it's loose in a lady who lingers, saying she is lost. And choking on hello. They are one person...*

I never bought the bullets. Instead, I braved the bike lane by his house on the way to the health food coop. Just to check on my gladiolas. The bulbs I'd planted to grow our home of love were blooming like rebellion. Someone had been watering them, and they burst in Krishna blue and fire orange.

That's when I burst like the flowers. I'd put my foot down, and I'd put my kickstand down. I skidded to a halt and parked my bike. His bike wasn't there, but his housemate's was. I told the housemate I needed to find my favorite skirt, which Jesus had torn off on our last day of worship. But really I was looking for that last piece of me still holding his thighs for dear life.

I climbed the creaky ladder to his bedroom. No invitation to cry about our childhoods helped me open the trapdoor. No erect, sacred scepter led the way. The attic seemed almost pathetic now, lit by a bare bulb. The cardboard over the window muffled the cars raining by. The Stradivarius lay naked under the leaky roof, warped but ready for our world tour.

Was this really the only church I'd ever worshipped in? Now there was only dust, the layers of our love screams sloughed off like so many dead fingernails. My favorite skirt was gone forever, as was the little pink hat. Stubs of joints littered the floor.

Suddenly I realized there were no rules. I could smash his Stradivarius if I wanted to. I could tear up the ugly yellow shirts and start a fire. Or I could dye his underwear green with forest moss, bear his skinny, big-footed child. I wanted to pray to release it all, but couldn't choose between two broken hallelujahs: "Fuck you" or "I love you."

I thought it would help to see it was all a dream, but it felt unbearably lonely to think I'd been wrong to love. I thought it would be easy to hate him, but it wasn't. "Not at all, not at all," I moaned as I rolled into a ball on the floor.

I half hoped the Prince would come home to find the lovesick princess in total abdication. He'd be wearing his white pirate bandana over his ringlets, and the black Sharpeed pirate boots. Like Jesus Depp. He'd cradle my face in his hands, call me Dark Eyes, and...

That's when I saw them. Balls of paper littered the floor, along with the joint stubs. They were opening like flowers, their petals pleading for my return. They were growing all over the floor, one for each time we'd made love. And they were watered with his tears.

"Dark Eyes, I'm sorry," said one. "I'm hurting," said another, "I can never play CSN again." Then, "I loved you too much" trailed off into scratch-outs, tear-stains, and another joint stub. *Gasping at glimpses of gentle true spirit, he runs, wishing he could fly, only to trip at the sound of goodbye.*

A halo formed over the bare bulb and the room felt close and cozy, like it used to. He did love me. He had just temporarily failed his training in how to be human, like all of us. As a man, he took too much credit for himself, just as I took too little as a woman. That's when I knew I could leave.

As a girl, I might have tried to love him more after that, to heal the wounded kitten. But I was older now, three whole months older. I'd taken Jesus as my personal savior. And Jesus was Me. The last piece of my soul nailed on the cross of his shoulder flew back to me. I closed the trap door, returning to the world solo and whole.

The world where my father's bathrobe still hangs as if he's in it. He still rules the family, breaking my mother's vases in various ways, but needing her desperately. I don't know why she stays, but maybe long ago she saw a birthmark under his beard that marked him as the Chosen One. Hopefully before he dies, paper flowers will grow from his bathrobe pockets.

MAGIC!

Sometimes a dog just keeps scratching at the door until you let him out; sometimes a story is a pony in a coral before a rainstorm, feeling energized by the pending thunder and lightning, leaping the fence. And sometimes a writer is ten-months-big in a nine-month-womb. Our "fivers" do their best to explain their own motives and inspirations, each one highly personalized.

But I have NEVER heard of a writer who is in it for the money.

What a writer wants, what our five authors here want, is *you.* An audience.

But if publication is so ethereal, and actually making a few dollars for your efforts a long shot at best, why even bother?

I will tell you why.

Several years ago very humble man approached me with a work in progress, a memoir of his time in Vietnam. The war left him addicted, poisoned by Agent Orange, crippled in body and spirit. Within a few pages of his manuscript, he shared this epiphany: "Twenty-seven years after I got on the flight home, I saw that Nam war was just *raw man,* spelled backwards. I'm pretty raw today."

Fred Rivera strapped himself into his chair as if it were the track he powered into battle a half a century ago, and bled out *Raw Man,* which won the Isabelle Allende Best New Fiction award when we published it in 2015. Central to the story, Herman Johnson, a string bean of a kid from Detroit and Fred's best friend, dies in his arms.

But that's not the story I want to tell. You can find that at *www.rawmanthebook.com.* It's what happened *after* we published that I need to tell you about.

As Fred recovered from the laceration of body and spirit, he developed his capacity to help other vets suffering from PTSD and became a counselor, saving the lives of suicide-prone combat soldiers. One such soldier Fred rescued was Sgt. John Marek, an Afghan vet, who, in appreciation for what Fred had done for him, decided to get a pencil etching of Herman Johnson's name from the Vietnam Memorial Wall in D.C.

But he couldn't find the name. And then he had the most peculiar thought: what if Herman didn't die? Sgt. Marek was no stranger to the fog of war, and after intense research, he found someone matching Herman's particulars living in Detroit. He apprised Fred of the situation, and asked if he should pursue the leads.

Fred, overwrought by the possibilities issued a response: "Stand down."

Fred kept a letter in his breast pocket for two weeks, and then, on impulse, sent it to the address Sgt. Marek had provided.

Three days later, Fred got the phone call...

"Fred?"

"Herman?"

Each thought the other had died.

A Word with You Press organized a GoFundMe campaign to reunite the two in the obvious location: The Vietnam Memorial Wall in our nation's capital.

Herman, who had been severely wounded in the battle Fred recreates in *Raw Man*, woke up in a field morgue to find his dog-tag between his teeth, the army equivalent of a yellow tag on the big toe. Yet, Herman was never awarded a Purple Heart.

Unbeknown to Herman, Fred worked tirelessly behind the scenes before their reunion, and General Guy Swan was on hand to preside over the event. "Sergeant: Read the orders."

A crisply uniformed Sgt. John Marek marched forward, and pivoted to address the curious, growing audience, with Fred and Herman to the side of the general.

"By order of the President of the United States, for wounds sustained in combat in Vietnam in 1969, the Purple Heart is hereby awarded Private First Class Herman Johnson."

Applause, spontaneous, and not a dry eye. I still get teary eyed thinking about it.

"Welcome home, son. It took us 47 years to right this wrong." After a salute, General Swan took Herman, still bewildered by what had just occurred, in his arms.

And now my point: None of this would have happened if Fred had not locked himself into his computer and told his story.

You will never know the effects of telling your story, until you tell it.

Reunited by the magic of the written word. Welcome home.

I've written for much of my post-second grade life, but now when I try to define the reason I write, I find the answer has been a moving target. I would have to admit that I write to remember, or perhaps more honestly, that I write to be remembered.

—Ben Angel
Associate Editor, A Word with You Press,
Wroclaw, Poland

Kristy Webster

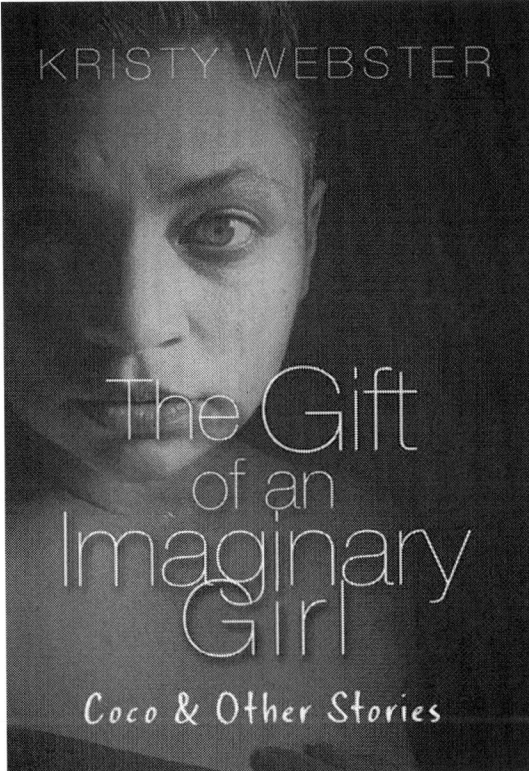

Published with A Word With You Press

...is the author of *The Gift of an Imaginary Girl, Coco & Other Stories,* published by A Word with You Press in 2015.

Her work has been featured in several online journals such as: *Lunch Ticket, Pithead Chapel, The Feminist Wire, Shark Reef Literary Magazine,* Pacifica Literary Review, *The Molotov Cocktail* and *Connotation Press.*

Her work is also featured in multiple print anthologies *A Woman's Work* and *Just Like a Girl* by Girl Child Press, and most recently, in *Two-Countries: U.S. Daughters and Sons of Immigrant Parents,* published by Red Hen Press in 2017.

Webster earned an MFA in Creative Writing from Pacific Lutheran University and a Masters in Teaching from Heritage University. She currently works as an elementary school teacher and part-time English professor.

Everyone should write, because the opposite of Depression is Expression.

Victor Villasenor
Best-selling author of
Rain of Gold, The Thirteen Senses and Burro Genius

Mike Stang

A bit like mustang, 1800–10, Americanism ; Spanish *mestengo,* stray or ownerless beast. That would be Mike.

If you're panning for pyrite as you sift through Mike's writings, all you're gonna find is gold. Sorry. His stories can be harsh, direct, but are always authentic. He has the capacity in his words to illuminate chasms of despair, and, through their often cathartic conclusions, make the pain of experiences more bearable. What Mike brings to this anthology, and all his writing, is the humility nurtured of his own tragic failures. Hey, we've all got them, but if a writer buries them, he knows enough to come back and water them from time to time. Mike's writing works, however, because he never plays the victim, just a very astute and self-aware literary hombre. I imagine in his younger days, hell, maybe even now, women want to run a comb through his desperado hair, tell him to stop riding fences.

I am always skeptical of writers who make themselves the hero of their every story. Is Mike the *anti*-hero of his stories? I don't think so. He is just an *honest* writer.

Paradoxically, that does make him a hero in my book. In *this* book.

I am proud to call him my friend, and the first to acknowledge he is a better writer than I will ever be.

Thanks for joining us, Mike.

Everybody's broken. That's how the light gets in.
Ernest Hemingway

THE ONE-OH-FIVE

Mike Stang

Private First Class Cage Hopper figured the diamond didn't just show up on its own but belonged to one of them high rich players that pulled up late at night in front of the clubs. High rich players don't wait in line to get their wrists stamped; neither do the pretenders that skunked on their daddy's arms lucky enough to be there.

Hopper was a ghost among them: what they *saw* was a jacked-up Viet Vet squatting on his haunches against the outside bricks. Token emotions around his neck and a cardboard sign directed anyone who cared he was ready for a handout.

What they didn't see was a sixty-seven going on a hundred and two ex-military, ex-milkman, with an ex-wife trying to fit in with veterans home from places like Afghanistan and Iraq. Sure they all had the universal brothers-in-sacrifice thing going, but the lingo was different ... the mindset. Like an old man frustrated by the new math, Hopper caught on to some of the slang but suspected a few smart-asses made fun of the crazies. They named him Sleeping Dragon. Hopper watched his back.

Fighting and dying in Fallujah and Kabul were *concrete* battlegrounds--not a rice paddy in sight. The theater was hard for Hopper to appreciate. His idea of field combat meant fighting under triple canopy trees that hid their dead since the second century; there, the soldier fought on some of the most beautiful and treacherous landscapes in the world. Vietnam was like that: where the sea stormed the land, a myriad of Paleozoic formations interrupted by pitons higher than the reach of the sky, and where bottomless drainage caves blurred the rules of how terrestrial planets evolved, cabalistic fog bound the past to a ghostly present. The culture had a spirit for everything.

Hopper couldn't move without knowing he had stepped on something. Trespassed on a life force that he couldn't see his only excuse. There were consecrated sites, locations of which only the hearts of Central Highland elders knew. They claimed these lands were made of jade and gold and protected by birds that looked like hawks with human extremities.

Before he lost his facility to read two sentences back to back, Hopper held an interest in Nam's biography. He toted a paperback inside his jacket that canvassed the different philosophies—a universe away from the legends of Middle Eastern genesis. Except for the killing, the wars were disjointed.

Hopper got by as best he could what with alcohol and illegals used against the feathery promises of government benefits that vanished behind a smokescreen of departmental vacancies. The old carney tricks he played down at the Veteran's Hospital no longer amused the secretaries. The private's capitulation and a dead-end trail of empty script containers pushed him towards the inevitable business end of a gun. He knew it was only a matter of time when the realization struck he had little else to lose. Kate, his wife of twenty years, left screaming into the night some thirty years ago. Left everything where it stood except for their daughter, Shalie, who she dragged behind her; his little girl's eyes pleaded with him to make Mommy stop. It wasn't long after that he dumped himself on the corner with all the other floaters. *After all*, Hopper told himself, *America sucked; you get what they want you to get—fucked!*

Hopper kept his pride in how he had served as he settled into his veteran's lifestyle. He thought about the close relationship with his lieutenant and about the help he gave to others of his unit so they might survive another day and about his legacy of making the best by God, goddam coffee in the field. Life on the lam had its moments, but they were nothing more than fleeting facades, memories designed to remind him he could still feel, if only for the moment. Then they were gone.

Hopper knew all veterans faced mental cancer. He could tell when the lights went out; soldiers who had given in to the totality of war walked around going through the motions until eventually they met their dead ends. Hooper used everything he knew from his military training. What was left of his intelligence, his imagination and the luck of the draw he kept that shit at bay.

~

The diamond appeared out of nowhere—like the beginning of a fantasy novel—on the sidewalk, hidden behind the veteran's left heel. For a moment Hopper felt giddy, out of body. He liked to think of himself in flashbacks as a human howitzer sitting up on a hill, the crew loading him up with a 105 shell, his mind locked on coordinates with enough firepower to finally do something about it. It made him feel good, feel right like fighting in Nam was right. Hopper didn't dwell on the politics too much; politics didn't last two bits in the field. One thing he knew for sure, however, was the rock never saw daylight when he slipped it into his coat pocket. What divine providence miracle kind of thing was going on Hopper was clueless, but nobody showed up yet to take his head off, and as the seconds ticked by, his breathing returned to normal.

Hopper hung around the club until the city swapped shadows for dawn; kept to his every day in case someone watched. There was enough pity-coin to grab a bus across town, but Hopper walked to the only person in his world he trusted, El-Tee Mac, his old lieutenant who rented a cold-water over on the Westside.

✎

The medevac chopper listed heavily towards the open doors on take-off, with body-bagged dead and wounded untethered. The load slammed around until you couldn't tell who was what. Hopper positioned himself at the back in a whirlpool of blood, tried to preserve what remained of his fragged right leg while he fended off another soldier's persistent attempt to crawl over him. It turned out the other guy was his lieutenant, sucking life through a chest wound. Mac was making to push himself out to the next hereafter, but Hopper got a hold of a boot; whispered to him stories of the old Boston they both grew up in—soda fountain girls, Southie football. In the end, they found each other laid out on stretchers in a mobile MUST unit saving each other's life by holding each other's hand, waiting for an airlift to Japan. The war was over for these two.

Pre-dawn fog crept along the hem at the bottom of the medical pod but did nothing to dispel the crippling heat that sapped the dying as they lay on their stretchers in grotesque formation. Most of them bled out unconscious not knowing they were heroes.

A pocket of unaccountable air shimmered between Hopper and the lieutenant. It glistened a silvery mist before the color of saffron took its place. Their eyes were aghast as they watched a monk's hooded robe dress a naked human female form. Morning shadows hinted at an ancient face and golden-glazed fiery-eyes. Hopper could not possibly have known he was staring at Vietnam's most revered goddess, Quan Am. She stood, however, before them a thief and a wanted subversive in the eyes of the modern day, for crimes against the state. Such as it always had been. Those who worshipped her or showed devotion within the thousands of pagodas in her name faced arrest; some tortured, some disappeared; all sacrificed without question but none of her stalkers remotely affected her mission. As perilous as her situation, she was fearless.

70

Events, as were seen and decided upon by an ancient council of trace beings that recognized leadership other than the last man standing, were about to change for Vietnam. Hopelessness was the face of evil, and the simple, divided humanity of north and south floundered in its panic. The compassion of East Asia and those who would wield it kept a new watch over its people whose cadaverous, supplicated arms cried out to the mystic to save their beloved country from extermination. The empty promises herald by the next revolutionary chiefs were no longer received as the law of the land. The very idea of unification was sacred and secret, passed from peasant to peasant until there was only one thing left to do. Steal back what was rightfully theirs—their country.

Quan Am had a plan...

A soothing lithesome hand took away the soldiers' pain and rocked them as if the queen mother cradled them at her bosom. Quan Am opened a channel in Hopper's mind. Showed him images of Vietnam's history he never discovered within the thin pamphlet passed around among the new troops by his government. Her Images portrayed how its citizens' blood fed foreign powers down through centuries of invasion. The soil saturated until all that would grow were fields of empty ammunition dumps. The visions cleared replaced by the robed figure's clear voice. Hopper received instructions. She pressed the Diamond of Annam into the private's hand while Lieutenant Mac succumbed to his wounds and died.

✌

"Fuck you. Show up with that, we both die." Lieutenant Mac ran around like a madman to close and drape the windows he could. Sweat shaped his back as Hopper remembered in the field.

"I was careful, El-Tee. Stole nothing. It found me."

"What, you think this a joke, Private? Gonna wake up tomorrow and laugh it off? Look at the goddam thing, you fool! That-a cartoon to you?"

The diamond sat on the lieutenant's table in the middle of scrunched up newspaper, folded flat. It didn't just sit there; it vibrated: phantom shards of aquamarine pulsed in different orbits around the gem's first brilliance, then dark, turning forest green.

"I taught you to steal, Private. Maybe we stole enemy rice, stole some weapons, snuck up on a few live ones and stole their lives, but that was war. I never taught you this."

"Didn't steal it, El-T, honest."

The lieutenant made it to the door as if under fire. Slowly he opened it and looked both ways for a long time before he grabbed Hopper by the back of the neck and threw him out, diamond and all. Neighbors emerged from other doors and threatened to call the cops on this guy who kept beating on the outside of the vacant apartment. Hopper didn't believe his only friend would drop him, not now, not when the diamond could do them some good. *What if I cashed it?* Hopper wondered what a million bucks looked like, maybe two; he had no idea. All he could think of was glitter and how the world would sparkle for them both.

For the life of him, the veteran couldn't understand why his lieutenant didn't want any part of that glitter. This was their chance to become something more than what society left for them. *We could patch our families back together—maybe,* Hopper thought. *Be a father to Shalie if she'd let me. Don't be stupid, you old fool, she'd never thi...well, maybe.* Hopper's hands started to shake. *School! I could go back to school.* The sixty-seven-year-old chuckled thinking he could return to research. *They'd call me Pops; I'd walk around in corduroys.*

Hopper ran down the stairs and all the way to the next bus stop no longer worried about being followed.

The nights were the worse. The way the city lights against a black sky full of stars reminded the veteran of tracer rounds, fired by gunships that flew invisibly above the battlefields; death's ghosts. The dark confused him, squeezed his stomach, knuckle-white. Tonight, though, would be different. *Okay, Mac's out,* Hopper said to himself. *I get that, I'll do this on my own. So what, I'm a loaded Howitzer on a hill; who's gonna fuck with that?*

The veteran knew he was up against impossible odds turning the stone to cash. He knew he would die in prison if caught but if there was a chance to get back his old life; show Kate, give Shalie everything she deserved, then why not? Anything was better than this.

⁓

The diamond weighed a fraction of those grenades Hopper used to snap to his web gear. He pulled it from his pocket and held it up. The city, the lights, and the bright stars lost their energy as if the jewel sucked everything into itself. The cuts danced in front of the veteran's mind and opened a miniature universe that was stunning. Strangely familiar, a tune played in his ears messaged from the bones buried beneath the hues of the Banyan Tree over eight thousand miles away.

MIA's and the dead always stand down, lost forever they rumor impatiently "Come back and dance," they whisper, "come back and dance on your brothers' graves." The unforgettable face of the woman monk formed in front of the veteran's own.

The monk, of course ...

A room locked with cobwebs fell open in Hopper's soul. He remembered the instructions from so long ago: *"You will carry this diamond to the West and lose it, forgetting you even possessed such a thing. The gem will find you again. Return it to me and place it in my hands the same way I am giving it to you now. This war will have ended. The time for unity and peace will be at hand. The people will need their seed to bring them together."*

~

The ghost of Samson, Hopper's point dog killed in action twelve days after he was assigned, showed up beside him on the sidewalk and stayed while the veteran's purpose clarified. The clock ticked down the time to go east. Hopper gave away his possessions to the other vets on the last day. Samson licked Hopper's hands. The soldier's eyes lit up to the sounds of a jungle no one else heard. Sixty-eight pounds of purebred told his master it was time to return to the end of the war.

~

United flew Hopper from Kennedy to Frisco. Korean Air got him to Hanoi, a city which staggered his imagination. He never thought of the people of North Vietnam as anything but stupid and downtrodden, assumed the enemy incapable of supporting their capital, but there, a state-of-the-art metropolis showed through the plane's windows.

Air Vietnam took him to Da Nang in a 60's era Soviet transport, squeezing under a last-minute magenta sky streaked with pure yellow. It was the second week in October; the monsoons were late but the motor scooters that jammed the squares, feverishly to get somewhere before the colors vanished, told of an imminent story. Standing in baggage claim pushed Hopper's memory into over-drive. People, places, and things he had touched or saw, spun time around and blurred the past to the present. The old familiar hundred-pound heat took up quarters at the back of his neck; Hopper's stomach wrenched the same old butterflies, the same old fears. He looked around for a handwritten sign with his last name on it ...

Reservations at the Dai a Hotel were simple. There was a message waiting for him at check-in, cautioning him not to unpack. The rented Rover would arrive at the entrance gate at 2:30. Mountain ranges soaring west showed pockets of the 21st century. A number of fat, South Vietnamese old ruling families, and a few western AWOL generals built their power compounds on top of the same hills that back in the late sixties, early seventies were backdrops dominated by the bloodiest battles fought between American infantry and the minions of the Vietminh.

The driver, a forty-year-old Montagnard named Jaa-Ntoor, whose ancestor's blood tracked back to the Degar village of Sar Luk, seemed unaffected by the presence of manned checkpoints. Eventually he left the mapped route altogether and traveled roads that Hopper thought the tribesman had built himself. The climb increased. Ridges and open-mouthed valleys disappeared below. Snaked rivers looked like wiggled pencils you saw from space. The mist thickened to clouds until the two men found themselves surrounded by a white sky. Jaa-Ntoor stopped the Rover.

"We walk," he said, and smiled a toothy, easy grin. With backpacks full of food and gifts the two men roped themselves together and climbed until the whiteness lost its brilliance to the coming night. Jaa-Ntoor guided Hopper to a cave, and over rare delicacies of roasted termite and smuggled Chinese Puerh tea, Hopper's nervousness left him.

"Who are you...really?" Hopper asked his host.

"I am but a Tracer. I have come to deliver you to Quan Am." Jaa-Ntoor eyed the old veteran respectfully. His silver goatee veiled a muscular body perfectly physical. His eyes reflected a mind capable of crossing the rivers between differential realities with the ease bestowed from his ancestors. Hopper thanked him for his service and made the slightest bow, honoring a leader.

"There are questions I would ask... " As Hopper spoke, he could feel the energy in him change. A nostalgia blossomed in his heart; a legacy of serving one's country in a time of war. Guilty for every kill shot. Only his lieutenant would understand. *What am I doing here,* Hopper asked himself, he looked around as if for the first time. *Serving a ghost, chasing a crazy woman's dream. I've gone nuts somewhere along the line.*

Jaa-Ntoor saw the veteran's struggles. "Wait for her," was all he said.

Hopper's energy shifted again. Drawn to the emergence of the buddhist priestess, in the middle of the cave. A full-length scarf of pure blue lay against her celibate ivory skin. Before Hopper, she closed her eyes and extended her left hand, the same one she used to bestow on him her country's salvation. In slow motion, Hopper closed his own eyes and dug out the Diamond of Annam. When he opened his eyes to give it to her, the Goddess showed a thousand left hands all waiting for the gem. Her smile encouraged him to choose one. Hopper looked over at Jaa-Ntoor, as if in a dream he was dipping an earthen clay cup into a bowl of mud that clarified to mash and then again to an alcoholic juice. The tribesman toasted Hopper and told him to believe that the truth of compassion ran through him. A furious storm arose and tore a hole in Hopper's stomach. His mind watched from several vantages as two Ao Dai dressed Vietnamese girls poured golden liquid into his wound. A star formed on the veteran's forehead, the light of which illuminated one of the goddess's arms. He took a breath and gave Quan Am the stone of Vietnam.

Quan Am shifted her eyes down to meet Hoppers', her body had grown to a giant size. "You are blessed, Private Hopper. I bow and call you *Bodhisattva.* My country's highest honor is to serve its people, thereby bringing them to peace, safe from confusion and pain. Because of you, Vietnamese peoples return to their paddies and continue to do what they have only wanted since our land separated from the ocean. Your sacrifices have not gone unnoticed, nor your wishes."

The scene fell away as Quan Am, the cave, the long road traveled and the dust of a veteran's life developed into memoir; written then published for Hopper to marvel at the glossy jacket before he set it on antiquity's shelf. Only Jaa-Ntoor remained by his side and offered a taste of the wine, commanding him to drink. A blend of ginger and cinnamon laid on his tongue and cleared and settled his body for what was to come.

Jaa-Ntoor disappeared and Hopper along with him. They emerged at the edge of a jungle before a valley that sprawled before them without end. Waist-high elephant grass the color of velvet sage concealed the Asian repository of war. Soldiers slowly materialized out from the steamy woods. Their march ripped currents of patterns pressed by the wind through the lea. Battalions of men advanced, as many a man as blades of grass. Rifles laid across the back of their shoulders loosely supported by sunburned arms, looped over barrels and butts. They kept coming easily; tolerant and good-humored.

These were the soldiers of the dead. Hopper knew them all, if not by name by family—they were his brothers. The old platoon moved forward, stopping to laugh and tell dirty jokes. They patted Hopper's back and hugged him; welcomed him back. El-Tee Mac was there. Samson sat at point, the forever soldier, and looked back at Hopper ready for patrol.

Jaa-Ntoor urged Hopper to join his men; give in to the allure lucid in his eyes. The smells and sounds of jungle fueled what Hopper felt inside; the only stored archive to offer any sense of home. *Funny,* Hopper thought, *the place I consider stable is an old war zone occupied by the ghosts I spent time with when they were men alive.*

The columns grew to legion strength; the men began to chant in a military beat, hummed by the soldiers and echoed by all soldiers since the beginning of time. The music rose from the valley floor past the gates of what soldiers knew, beyond thresholds they would never understand. They were soldiers after all.

Private First Class Cage Hopper chanted and danced right along with the best of them, the happiest he had ever been.

When they came to a patch of high ground the men halted and lifted Hopper up, passing him above their heads to the top of a hill. They welded his arms on to a five-inch cylinder, eleven feet long. His body bolted to the front end of a tank. Hopper's eyes became scopes displaying longitude and latitude in progressive dashed patterns. A crew of "Gun Bunnies" inserted in his case a one-oh-five then shut and locked the backfire cap tight. Private Hopper's ears received a radio signal—fire at will.

But then again, no. The star that formed on his forehead from his conversion at the hands of Quan Am shone forth with a strength of a million candle lights. He searched the mountains and saw no enemy, the valleys peaceful, the shores idyllic. Clouds of war dissipated and centuries of struggles dissolved. No longer a reason to realize his draggled flashbacks, the veteran disengaged from the war machine.

From the sky fiery crystals released across the land, ending Vietnam's malignancy to harmless pollen. Like fairy dust, it filtered down to seed a carpet of wildflowers over the forest floor. The Diamond of Annam then rose steadily above all else, an elemental treasure it blazed like the sun and connected to the private's star. Each soldier's heart was touched with a healing spark, lifting them free of their earthly bonds; new bodies and souls to the ether.

Throughout the fields of Southeast Asia, weapons were lost. A thunderous clang heralded in the era of peace, the sound to end all wars. The veteran stood, his arm around his lieutenant's shoulder. Jaa-Ntoor stood before them. Together they walked into the future and disappeared.

Ed Coonce is truly a renaissance man.

(Men, actually.)

One persona is simply not enough to keep the lid on his Id. So he has enlisted the aid of two (that we know of) alter egos to direct the traffic of his creative flow on East Hell Boulevard: The white lab-coated Dr. Hannover— ever ready to deliver a baby or a punch line, and the effusive, illusive, often obtrusive good 'ole boy, Billy Bob, who each help him make the satirical lyrical.

But there is more to Ed, as I have learned over ten years, than just our shared reverence for seventh-grade humor. He can't be constrained by mastering just one medium: He is an accomplished playwright, stand-up comic, social critic, visual artist and actor. If you've read the biography we've posted, you know he has a lot of material to work with. *5x5* displays only one aspect of this multi-talent artist. As I sit composing this, if I gaze at the opposite wall, I am inspired by one of his paintings, as distinctive in style as his writing.

Black and White

THE MATRUSHKA INCIDENT

Ed Coonce

Bobby fell asleep after a night of drinking and partying at the Hunchback Inn. He didn't go home, he apparently just passed out on the dance floor.

He awoke the next morning standing upright in a cartoon forest. A bluebird chirped on a nearby tree branch. Glockenspiel music tinkled in the background.

"Dammit," thought Bobby, faintly remembering the previous evening's debauchery. "How in hell did I end up here?"

"Here" happened to be a large oblong egg-shaped object, a matrushka. He was nearly six feet tall, flat painted features, no legs, and inside him were two others, one nesting within the other.

Bobby could feel the other two stirring inside his shell, and each of them was murmuring and babbling something he couldn't quite hear till they began yelling.

"Where the fuck am I?" shouted matrushka number two. His name was Billy.

Inside Billy, Tommy, the third matrushka, screamed. "God help me!! Aaauuuggghhhh!! I'm in Hell!!.....sob!"

"Calm down everybody!" yelled Bobby, trying to be calm. He couldn't move his head, he noticed he had no legs either, just painted-on ones. He tried to move, rocking back and forth. Billy and Tommy did the same, at the same moment. Bobby toppled over, his shell popped open at the waist and Billy popped out.

"Fuck!" yelled Billy, when he saw Bobby and his surroundings. "What the hell is this?" He tried rocking across the forest floor, but fell forward, tumbling over Bobby's lower half. His own shell opened up and out rolled Tommy. Whimpering, Tommy continued rolling on down the trail and over a cliff. He screamed all the way down, till he landed, shattering himself into a hundred pieces on the jagged rocks at the bottom.

"Well, that was interesting," remarked Bobby, who was known for his level-headedness.

"What are we gonna do, man?" cried Billy.

The bluebird took off then, chirping until it was out of sight. The background music stopped.

Does it ever get dark in a cartoon forest? thought Bobby. He shuddered. He couldn't close his painted-on eyes. He wanted to throw up.

Professor Hanover Klingst and RuPaul, his laboratory assistant, watched the matrushkas on the computer screen. His latest experiment was a success, they had succeeded in placing humans into a real computer game. He was biding his time, waiting for the right moment to implement Phase Two.

Only one problem, though: no redos. The shattered matrushka Tommy was gone for good, he wasn't going to be able to join the other two in the next part of the game, the part where they are turned into My Little Pony characters and turned loose in the middle of the movie Braveheart. Professor Klingst was about to realize his fondest dream; Twilight Sparkle carrying Mel Gibson into a medieval battle.

I am often asked "What is fiction?" Chief Broom explains it in the first few pages of *One Flew over the Cuckoo's Nest*:

If I told people what really went on in here, they'd think I was crazy. But it's the truth, even if it didn't happen.

And I am often asked, "What is *literary* fiction?"
Even easier to answer: "*The Old Man and the Sea* is not about fishing."

Thornton Sully

BIRD WATCHING

Jon Tobias

Frank and Old Bubs, formerly, Bubs, both sit on the couch and watch tv. Both of their bellies stick out a little as she likes to sit on her butt when next to him. Her tongue hangs out of the side of her mouth, and she pants a little, feigning interest in what is happening. In return he gently strokes the back of her head. She enjoys this so much that she looks sleepy and drunk. He sips his morning coffee with his free hand.

"You seem happy today, old girl."

She turns her head towards him and continues panting.

He stands and walks to the kitchen to get her food. She doesn't come. Instead, she moves from her upright position to a lying one and tucks her front paws under her chin.

"Bubs. Come eat."

Only her eyes move to his location. He thinks he should have purchased one of those stair things he saw at the store. It is on of those spoil your pet things for dogs who have trouble getting on and off couches and beds, but he decided lifting her on and off is better. She only weighs about thirty pounds now, and the weight and warmth of holding a thing you love feels better than pushing around a small set of stairs. He thinks maybe it makes her feel welcome that he puts in the extra effort. Never mind that his forearms are covered in bandages from her dull claws tearing away at his skin. It's not her fault. It's his for getting old.

Old Bubs is all he has left, but more and more lately that doesn't seem like it will be the case for much longer. Frank can tell her back legs are getting weaker by the day. Soon they may not work at all. He is relieved a little in understanding this because after she goes, he can go. It's not that Frank wants to die. He just misses his wife, and with Old Bubs gone, all he will have to do is wait out the days. He hopes they won't be long. He hopes the stories about loneliness killing a man are true.

Frank lifts Old Bubs off the couch. She is limp in his arms, tightening up just before he sets her down. In the process she lets loose a bandage on his arm and blood trickles down to his fingertip. She walks to her bowl showing no signs of the pain her hips are in, and Frank says out loud that she is such a strong girl as he wipes himself with a paper towel.

In the same way that dogs and their owners start to look alike, Frank knows that Old Bubs adopted her strength from his late wife. He knew she was sick, but they both had hope. He didn't even realize she was losing the fight until she started teaching him how to do things like making the brussels sprouts just right. It is his favorite dish. She always went heavy with the butter and garlic before baking them. He finally admitted to himself he was going to lose her when she ordered him a new reading lamp and pajamas to replace the holey ones he had worn for years. Lastly, she bought them a dog, a little tan colored mutt from the pound. She was something for him to take care of after. She was a reason to live a little longer. What hurt most was that his wife was the strongest woman he knew, and he always said that to her. They had no children, so for two years after they got Bubs, it was just the three of them.

His wife's name? Her name was Elizabeth. Is Elizabeth. But he called, calls, her Birdie.

It takes Old Bubs some time to eat her food as she takes breaks every few bites. She sighs during some of these breaks. They are big, breathy sighs that draw attention as if she were a spoiled child who is upset and wants someone to ask about it.

"You don't have to finish it, old girl."

She sighs again and goes back to eat more. Frank finishes his coffee over the sink, so he can watch her.

Old Bubs gives up, leaving food in the bowl for Frank to throw away. He puts on his favorite baseball cap, thinking he might walk her, but she looks up at him with a sadness in her eyes that says, "I can't."

"You're such a strong girl."

He pats her head, gently scratching the space between her eyes. She tries to sit while he pets her, and she lets out a soft whimper.

"One more good afternoon, Old Bubs. Then we'll call it."

In his head, it seemed like the best thing to do. He would spend one more day with her before the pain got worse and her legs gave out completely, then he would put her out of her misery. If it were him, he would want the same.

Frank opens the sliding glass door that leads to the patio and sits at the table on the porch. He lights up the one cigarette he allows himself a day. He was never able to quit entirely, and when people asked about just the one, he would respond, "I'm not trying to live longer. Just long enough."

When Old Bubs was just Bubs, she spent entire mornings in the backyard with Frank and Elizabeth scaring the birds that lived in the tree. There wasn't enough room for her to run. The backyard has mostly enough room for the small covered porch, and the tree in the back, but her jumping and clawing and barking at the base was enough to scare any birds up there.

Today, Frank finishes his cigarette before she makes it outside to join him.

"There's my strong girl."

Frank looks to the tree, pats Old Bubs on the head and says a prayer, "Birdie, set some space aside up there. It's been long enough. I miss your smile. I miss making you mad and laugh at the same time. I miss the way your shoulder feels on my forehead. Also, it's your turn to look after our old girl."

Old Bubs slowly heads toward the tree, limping slightly as she goes. She looks up to see if there are any birds in it. There are, but she lies down instead, places her head on the ground and tilts her eyes towards the branches.

"I think that will be a good place to bury you."

Frank knows animals usually find some quiet place away from their human families to pass. Sometimes they get far enough away that people might think their pet ran off, which in a way, is kinder. Sometimes it's nice to leave someone with a little hope that something might come back to them.

While getting his gun out of the safe, Frank thinks, *she loves vanilla ice cream.* For a moment he can't remember which *she* that is. It doesn't matter. A treat is a treat. Ice cream also means one last car ride.

He leaves the safe on the kitchen counter and goes outside to get Old Bubs, then carries her to the car. She winces as he picks her up. He places one arm under her butt and another on her back. She buries her face into his neck and sighs again. It is a humble sigh that says, *thank you,* and, *I love you.*

He turns the radio on and rolls the windows down. She smiles a dog smile and pants in the back seat but does not go to stick her head out the window like she used to. She whines as he leaves the car, finally mustering the strength to look out the window as Frank goes into the store.

Coming back, from the distance of the store entrance, Frank swears he can see her shoulders working suggesting that her front paws are dancing. She even whips her head back, something he always thought meant, *hurry up!*

"There's my strong girl."

He places a few scoops of vanilla ice cream into a bowl, taking a few bites for himself before putting the pint into the freezer. Old Bubs eats the ice cream much faster than she ate her breakfast. Maybe it is the excitement over the treat, but she seems like the young dog she used to be with more energy than him and Birdie could handle. They always had a carpet littered with stuffing from toys, a coffee table that never seemed to be clear of dog hair no matter how much Frank cleaned it, and a wet nose to the cheek every time they were low enough for her to get close.

As soon as she laps up the last bit of cream from the sides of the bowl, Old Bubs collapses to the kitchen floor like a marathon runner crossing a finish line. She looks up at Frank without moving her head.

"I know the feeling, strong girl. Let's get you outside." Frank scoops up Old Bubs one last time. Her back leg slips a little, scratching his arm. He adjusts it before noticing the blood he accidentally wipes on her fur. He rests her under the tree. She watches the birds as they tweet and flutter amongst the branches.

Frank wraps his forearm with a rag and begins digging. It hurts his hands though the soil is soft. It hurts his back. Frank starts to sweat. After each slam into the earth, lifting the shovel back up feels like reeling in an anchor by hand. Whether she knows what he is doing or not, Old bubs begins to help Frank dig. She lies at the edge of the hole and pulls back dirt with her front paws.

Upon seeing her dig her own grave, Frank begins to cry. He digs faster. His body becomes a machine that only knows how to steadily remove dirt from the ground. The movements are mindless. The rag on his arm might as well be soaking up oil instead of his own blood. His face might as well be a broken radiator, dripping coolant instead of tears. Not knowing how to comfort him, Old Bubs moves slowly to Frank and presses her head into his knee. Frank finally stops.

Without being asked, Old Bubs lies down in her soon to be grave, and instead of looking to Frank, she looks to the tree full of birds. In that moment Frank decides that dying is not being able to have or do the things that make you happy. It isn't outrageous things like trips out of the country or going to parties. It isn't any of the things you have to spend money on to do. It is being able to kiss your wife before you go to bed at night. It is being able to scare birds and then watch them fly above your head. It is the sound of their wings. It is the way Birdie says, "I love you," as if it were the perfect response to everything.

Frank wipes his face, and then grabs his gun from the kitchen. Old Bubs still lies peacefully in her hole staring at the tree. Frank takes the safety off and stands over her. He aims the gun towards the sky and fires twice. Birds fly out of the tree, chirping wildly, shaking the leaves, causing small shadows to dance over the two of them. Old Bubs, who didn't flinch at the shots, smiles a dog smile and sits up a little. She even lets out a low bark.

"I'm not a writer, but..."

The number is now six. I started keeping count after three.

That is the number of times over the years that the first words from someone, upon discovering I am a publisher and editor, are "I'm not a writer, but ..." and then the not-a-writer admits they have 300 pages of manuscript clawing through the glass of their computer screen. You do not need the validation of a published work to persuade me you are genuinely a writer: you only have to write.

Thornton Sully
Editor in Chief of *A Ww YP*

I write because I am a slave's dream come true, and in the Library of Babel, I cry out their echoes.

Tiffany Vakilian
President, San Diego Book Awards
Associate Editor at *A Ww YP*

The test of good fiction is that we want it to be true, even though we know it isn't.

Derek Thompson
Author of the Thomas Blade detective series
Contributing Editor at *A Ww YP*

Peggy Dobbs had a green thumb.

Mold and mildew bloomed gloriously on the yellowing pages of short stories composting in the bottom draw of her bedroom dresser in Alabama.

Then one day while she was gardening, her nephew, Brian Harrison, suggested the crop might do better if it saw the light of day. He helped her with the transplant, transcribing the imprint of leaden keys from an old Smith Corona into the fertile fields of a laptop, and sending it to *A Word with You Press* as an entry into the contest *du jour* we sponsored at the time.

As Peggy got feedback, which is standard when people post their stories and contest entries, she discovered—WE discovered—that her writing was really quite good. Her home-spun stories of life with her beloved husband, Homer, became a staple in what Peggy pegged as our "playground." She became to our website what Grandma Moses was to painting. She quickly progressed under Brian's guidance from learning how to send an email to learning how to send an attachment. From that point onward, there was no stopping her.

About the same time on the left side of the continent, Miryam Howard started submitting her own stories and contest entries, also engaging to read, and well received. As they started commenting on each other's stories, they realized that they had much more in common than just the satisfaction of writing. Private emails exchanged between them nurtured a wonderful friendship. They started by sharing recipes and later sharing their hearts. At 82, Peggy left us too soon. Which reminds me of the quote that introduces our webpage in Europe, *Positively Prague*: "Let us hurry to love people, they depart so quickly." (Jan Twadorski, Polish Poet).

Miryam Howard is one of the many friends that Peggy left behind, and their bond was legendary—also emblematic of what this site accomplishes: uniting diverse people for the common good of self-expression. Peggy, the born-again Baptist from Alabama and Miryam, the rabbi's wife from the Pacific Northwest were not going to let any cultural differences stand in the way of a good friendship.

Peggy's daughter, Niki Dobbs Dambro, was good enough to let us know that belonging to the *A Word with You Press* community which Peggy helped to create gave her strength, purpose and pleasure in her sunset years.

Brian Harrison continues to stop by the playground from time to time, when he is not busy teaching English in South Korea or other parts of the world. Miryam and husband Baruch have followed their dream, and have immigrated to Israel, and I have followed my own dream to live in central Europe as a digital nomad, collecting stories here and there, and persuading others, maybe you (?) that your stories are the best way for us to connect to one another, as stories connected the wife of a Rabbi and a born-again Christian.

About Kristy

Kristy...I love you.

I have never known anyone as naked as Kristy Webster. She writes as if she has nothing to lose, and her brash honesty allows me, as a reader, to indulge in my own introspection: if she can do it, so can I. She does it with the world watching; I do it privately.

But unlike Kristy, I tend to edit myself for public consumption. I fabricate a persona that I then present to the world: Kristy *reveals* an unedited person to the world. A *good* writer is a successful manipulator, anticipating what combination of words and phrases will elicit a pre-desired response. A *great* writer, is Kristy Webster.

I am not as fearless as she is. Few writers are.

I do not over-intellectualize the production process. I try to keep it simple: Tell the damned story.

Tom Clancy

The only time I believe in God is when I think he is punishing me.

Kristy Webster

AN UNBEAUTIFUL LIKENESS
(Fiction)

Kristy Webster

Once, I heard a voice. The voice came from somewhere inside, but it still felt invasive. It wasn't mine, but it wanted to be. I felt those thoughts and those words throttle in my throat, vibrate through to the back of my neck. The voice said I didn't belong, not in my life and not in this world. The voice said that the only way to unveil my true reality was to die. If I were to die, I would wake up in the place I belonged I would come to know my real home. The voice spoke in an urgent tone, concerned and frantic. I decided to drown myself. I was five years old.

I have grown accustomed to people not believing me. Even my mother who said I had not heard a voice, but that I was hyperactive due to eating too many Fruit Loops. The sun and the clouds competed outside our window, and I spread out on the floor trying to understand, attempting to process what was expected of me. I played a game, rolling on the floor, chasing after the sunlight and trying not to touch the shadows.

It was a Friday and this is important. All Fridays of my childhood were important. The whole day ached with labor pains, as I knew we would be going to the *Salon del Reino*, the Kingdom Hall of Jehovah's Witnesses. It wasn't uncommon for me to suffer from constipation on meeting nights. Friday nights were shadows, too.

Our walls were false wooden panels, almost waxy looking. If you pushed or knocked on them hard enough, they would give a little and you would feel strong when you weren't strong at all. And as I prepared for another dreaded Friday night, I picked up a permanent black marker, and attempted to write my name on the paneling. The K and the R were backwards, and I didn't finish. Writing and reading in English confused me and made me feel stupid. Even writing my name hurt my guts. I've explained to the few people I've told this story to, that this was my suicide note. I had not heard the word suicide yet, at least, I don't think I had. But I knew I was planning to say goodbye. I knew I wanted to wake up. I believed the voice.

For years afterwards, I believed the voice was God, even though the voice was indisputably feminine, and our faith prohibited the idea of a female God, even considered it deeply sacrilegious.

After dinner, my mother drew me a bath. Hot baths have always been my refuge. The hotter the better. I tested myself, what I could take, watched the bottom half of my legs turn bright red. Eventually my body would adjust to the temperature of the water and I felt satisfied, like I had proved something.

I wondered how long it would take to drown. But first I enjoyed my bath. I relaxed, peacefully accepting that this wasn't real. It was only a dream. All of it. And death wasn't death, but a choice, to wake up to everything real, whatever that might be. I made a few test runs, holding a shampoo bottle like a barbell over my neck. But the door opened. My mother checked on me. My mother who seemed real. Very real. My mother's hands that always smelled like bleach or laundry soap. My mother in her house coats and rollers.

What if the voice was wrong? Then what? What if dying only lead to darkness? I was raised to believe in Satan the Devil. I was raised to believe that the Devil was a trickster, constantly trying to rip us away from Jehovah God, to sabotage our Faith. Her voice was beautiful, but I was taught that Lucifer was beautiful. The voice was female, but I was taught that Satan could speak through serpents, and that he was the Father of the Lie. And if the voice was wrong, I would never see my mother again, and my mother would be without me too. She would wonder why on earth I left her.

I sat up. I decided I would stay in the pretend place that might not be pretend, because the love I felt for my mother was real. It had to be.

In my late twenties I told this story to my Jamaican psychiatrist. He laughed. He said, "Children don't know about death. I don't believe you." He was also frustrated with me for grieving a pregnancy that I had terminated and mocked me for thinking I had a drinking problem. "Alcohol works," he said.

My memory is marred with gaps, periods of times that feel like drunken blackouts, and some of them literally were. But key moments, life defining moments, remain clear, sometimes painfully so. Sometimes beautifully so.

But I was always the five-year-old girl in the tub. I mean that, I flirted with my demise. I hurt myself, wondering if the voice would lead me somewhere. The voice never came back and it would take decades, for me to understand who that voice belonged to.

I grew up believing in black and white, good and evil, God and Satan. I believed things I didn't want to believe. I believed in things that hurt my stomach and made me cry and made me want to disappear. The ugliness in the scriptures, the terrifying commitment to the unknowable. But angels were different. Angels I could believe in. Angels made sense to me. My mother told me I was a gift from Jehovah God, and I took this to mean I was angel, not a human. And later wondered if that was the real life and place, I belonged in. My mother told me that angels are always watching and protecting us because we were part of the true religion of Jehovah's Witnesses. Always, I thought. Angels were always watching.

I spent a disproportionate amount of time on the toilet as a young child, suffering from constipation. My bottom would bruise. I felt desperate and terrified. Then I would think about the angels. The angels are watching me sitting on the toilet. I was convinced that the angels would not show themselves if my eyes were open. So I closed my eyes and reached my arms out, trying to feel for an angel. I had a picture in my mind of a golden, petite male angel. A stoic, quiet angel. I was so embarrassed.

The same psychiatrist who was convinced I was a liar also told me I should go into psychiatry. I asked him why and he said, "Because you have empathy. Do you realize what a small percentage of humanity is capable of true empathy?" And I didn't understand him. I was still angry that he wouldn't believe me. He also told me it was a good thing I was smart, though I didn't feel smart. He said, "If it wasn't for your intelligence, you'd be in a straitjacket." He was referring to the little girl on my couch who wasn't there.

My sons were with their father. I woke up from a nightmare, and there she was sitting on my purple couch. Her eyes blinked loudly like a scary doll. She was beautiful and I knew she was mine. But she disappeared and I knew she was like that voice, there, but not really there. A ghost of my own imagination.

I would have multiple hallucinations, both visual and auditory throughout my early thirties. I drank to make them go away. But I always knew, they weren't real. I had learned not to believe what I saw, what I heard. I came to think of my hallucinations as dull, annoying headaches. I would shut my eyes and take a deep breath. Then I would drink. And drink. And drink. And that was the elixir, the potion that spirited them all away.

It would be another four years before I was properly diagnosed and put on the appropriate medications and the hallucinations went away for good. Now that I've been on these meds for over a decade, I also believe that they will never come back even without the medication. And maybe that sounds I, but I think what I was experiencing was my mind generating my fear and confusion into visual specters. I believe that my brain was trying to fill in the gaps and urge me out of any complacency.

I had not heard the voice of God. I had not been in the presence of angels. But six days ago, I checked my son into a treatment center. He's only two years younger than I was when I was committed for eight days to a psychiatric ward. The emergency room, the same one where I threw a clipboard at a nurse, where the staff had to force me to drink charcoal to soak up the pills and make me vomit. And I made myself believe that the voice from all those years ago, was my own, my own to accept or refuse, and all those times I came back for air were preparing me for this moment: a son created in my image, maybe haunted by my mishaps, a hopelessness I understood, an echo I recognized. And I told him to be strong. Gave him tough love instead of holding him close the way I should have. As if it were contagious. As if I had not been the first carrier.

We are so much alike, he says.

I know, I say. What are we looking for? I ask.

We want so bad to be loved until nothing hurts anymore.

And then the voices, all voices in all the world, went silent, and the wordless room filled with the ghosts of tired efforts. Until finally, we laughed and split all the quiet in two.

We're past the age of heroes and hero kings...most of our lives are basically mundane and dull, and it's up to the writer to find ways to make them interesting.

John Updike, Writer's Digest

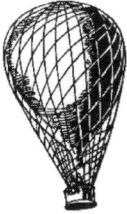

A SHORT TRIP

Jon Tobias

The tracks end at the base of the mountain where someone painted a tunnel large enough a train could pass through, were it real. The stone the tunnel was painted on had been carved flat to make the smooth surface ideal for the brushwork needed to create the effect. If you were to stand on the tracks at any point from where the station started all the way to the tunnel itself, you would swear it was real. The dead animal bodies on the ground in front sometimes give it away.

At the opposite end of the tunnel, about a mile outside the trading town known as Old-Water, a small wooden platform was built to serve as a station by men who would not say who they worked for nor why they were building it. They did not know. What mattered was that they got paid.

The train was built on site as well. Piece by piece, the parts were unloaded from crates and put together on top of the tracks after they were laid. The finished product was a train with a single passenger car, painted burgundy with gold plate over all the metal parts. The gold was so polished that whatever happened to be in front of it reflected perfectly.

The last thing to go up was a booth the same size as an outhouse. There it sat for months. To the community it was an eyesore that no one knew how to get rid of. To the children, it was a mystery.

〜

"Papa? Is anyone going to get to ride that train," Annie asks, wiping her hands on a dirty, light blue dress.

Timothy, a tall man with a big, graying beard sets down the feed bag he is carrying over, kneels down, spits on a handkerchief and wipes off her face.

"I don't think it goes anywhere, but maybe someone at some point will."

"Can I?"

"We'll see."

She smiles at the idea of being able to ride a train and skips the last few feet to the wagon that will take them back to their farm.

"It probably goes so much faster than this wagon."

"I believe it does, little girl." He pats her on the back to signal to hop up to her spot on the wagon.

"Make the wagon go fast, Papa!"

"Not today. Not with all we're hauling."

Annie sighs through her nose and slams her chin to her chest. Her father tugs on reins, and the horse starts its slow trot to the road out of town.

"Mama would have let me go fast, and she would have tried to get me a ride on the train."

"Mama is in heaven, and when you get up there with her you can ride as many trains as you want with Jesus himself as the conductor."

"I want to go to heaven now, then."

"You got to get as old as your mama was in order to get in. No little girls allowed. Especially cryin' ones."

"How come you're not there then?"

"I have to look after you until you're old enough."

Annie thinks about what heaven must be like while staring out at the parked train.

"There's a man," she shouts, "out by the train." Her shrill voice startles the horse as well as causes passersby to turn their heads in the direction of the station.

Though not much can be made out from the distance of town, it is clear there is a man, and he is strangely tall. He flaps his arms wildly and paces back and forth in long strides.

"Let's go, Papa!"

"We have too much to do at the farm."

"Please!"

"I have no money for a ride on a train, girl. The answer is no." Timothy, thinking the conversation is over, looks out towards the station. The man out there gives him an uneasy feeling. The man reminds Timothy of a sheet on a clothesline during a strong wind. Only, in this case, the wind is coming straight up out of the ground.

Annie jumps from the wagon. Her father reaches over to grab her but catches nothing. The horse pulling the wagon is too slow and has too much to maneuver around to get out of town fast enough. He abandons the wagon, but Annie is already far ahead of him. She will most likely reach the platform before he reaches her. Her blue dress bounces as she runs past the tall man and through the carriage door. Too late – by the time she boards, Timothy can do nothing to stop it.

Annie sticks her head out the window, "I'm on a train, Papa," and blows him a kiss. She has a smile on her face that Timothy hasn't seen since her mother was alive. Through the fear for her safety, he feels a little guilt, maybe he didn't do enough to make her happy.

Running, Timothy tackles the man at the legs, seeing he's balancing up on planks of wood. He hits the ground hard enough that Timothy is sure a few of the man's ribs cracked. Timothy then notices that above the black coat the man is wearing, his face is perfectly shaven and painted white.

"Stop the train!"

The man says nothing.

"Stop the train."

The man stares at Timothy as if the words are foreign to him. Timothy scours the platform for anything that might stop the train. Something to signal the conductor. Besides the bench, the empty ticket booth and the two of them – nothing.

Before he can do anything else, Timothy hears the crash of the train against the painted wall of the mountain.

Through tears and screams, Timothy lunges at the man who is still on the ground and begins punching him in the face. Wet slabs of meat dropped on a wood floor. His fists become painted, white and red, as he slams them down, over and over. The man coughs up teeth and thick blood onto the platform.

Timothy, through sobs, begins asking, "Why?"

After a moment, the man laughs in a way that makes Timothy feel stupid. He says, "Because I had the money to do it and no one stopped me," then rolls over and passes out.

People from town are already at the wreck. Some are there out of curiosity. Some are looting parts of the train. Timothy joins them, begins to search for Annie's body.

CHARLES AND CORDELIA

Ed Coonce

Charles, an ambitious entrepreneur, was no longer amused. He and his girlfriend Cordelia had reached a boiling point in their relationship in the early spring. Snow still lay scattered in the hollows of the Parisian streets and he was, as usual, worrying about their lack of income.

Cordelia was a Prancersize instructor and parlor magician who hired herself out for weddings, Bat Mitzvahs, and assorted gatherings. Her sleight of hand and prestidigitation skills were slipping, however, her act had deteriorated to nothing more than vague misdirection that tricked no one.

Charles confronted her.

"Face it, Delia!" Charles told her in a condescending tone. "Your magic is terrible! You're not fooling anyone!"

"No, look." she replied, anguished. She pulled a doily from the sofa, held it up, and waved one hand, then pulled a flower from under the cloth, a rotting rose with its stem broken and its petals nearly all gone.

"See?" said Charles derisively. "You're hurting our bottom line!"

They bantered about for a bit and decided to get Cordelia some professional assistance. They would consult Chriss Angel.

Chriss came by to impart what wisdom he had. He told Cordelia that all she had to learn was how to disappear and show up somewhere else, in another costume. She agreed, with a sweet smile and a slight wink from her left eye.

Charles didn't like the looks the two of them were exchanging. After Chriss left, he voiced his suspicions.

"You were coming on to him!" He pointed his finger at the door, in the direction Chriss had left.

She slapped him hard, then gave him a piercing, manic, paralyzing evil eye until he apologized.

"Sorry," he said.

Cordelia returned to practicing, tossing the doily and the decaying rose in the kitchen compactor. She left the house and crossed the street to the park, where a group of schoolchildren were playing kickball.

She waved one hand imperially, and a pet chihuahua disappeared from the grasp of a nearby young girl, leaving the youngster disoriented and tearful.

The dog reappeared moments later, materializing in the undergarments of a rotund genteel Spaniard walking on the Place de Catalogne. The astounded gentleman pulled the barking and biting pooch from his trousers and tossed him into an alley. The Spaniard suffered a rather nasty bite to one testicle, forcing him to hobble into a corner drug store, where he received a salve and a stern warning from the druggist.

"I would suggest a leash, monsieur," said the druggist.

Cordelia, meanwhile, was emboldened by this small success. "It works," she told herself.

Back at the house, she gathered a few belongings and her best frock, stuffed them into a round suitcase, and told Charles goodbye.

"Whatever," he responded.

She once again waved her hand and faded into nothingness while Charles was intently reading the financial pages of Le Monde.

Cordelia materialized moments later at La Caféothèque, where Chriss Angel had already seated himself. Excited, they ordered desserts, she, a puff pastry in the shape of a starfish, and he, a thin sliver of key lime pie. When they had finished, and before the waiter had brought them their bill, they both disappeared forever.

Charles spent the next two weeks secluded in the house, listening over and over to his dreariest Charles Aznavour records.

Laura Elizabeth

...is the writer of our five I most want to kick in the ass. I am constantly having to cajole, coerce or intimidate her into writing something. And yet, when she does, the heavens open up and a band of angels sings *Hallelujah* (Handel's, not Cohen's). She has no idea how good she is, and that she has no right to deny the world of her talents.

Many of us can recall childhood and adolescence (pronounced *add a lesson*) and write about it. What Laura can do is *become* a child, untainted by knowledge of the ways of the world, and share that experience with the vocabulary and insights of a warm and intelligent adult. Because of her writing, I can *understand* the crushing feminine devastation of young love gone bad, or a little girl betrayed by neglectful or insensitive adults.

I can't read anything Laura sends me without reading it four or five times, shaking my head in disbelief that anyone could be that good. Because we have published *5x5*, you don't have to take my word for it.

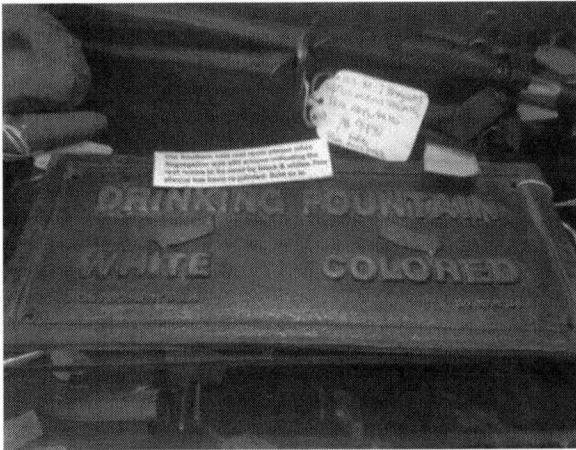

Of the fifty-plus contests we've sponsored over the years, none inspired such fierce passion as "The Drinking Fountain." I found a plaque in an antique store in Northern Idaho forged in Montgomery, Alabama in July 1931, that bore witness to ugly.

Writers were asked to respond to the plaque (which later morphed into the trophy) by recalling their own experience with racism, either as victim, perpetrator, or passive observer. Laura's entry, *A Salute,* was placed first by Pulitzer Prize-winner and friend Jonathan Freedman.

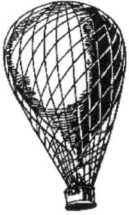

A SALUTE

Laura Elizabeth

At my grandparent's house, a clown pillow always waited, fluffed just for me. But I couldn't rest easy. Grandpa taught me to shuck corn under the blue-grey gaze of Lake Erie. Maybe he even held my hand. But above the guest bed, a glass case displayed the swords of the men he'd killed. They hung above the smiling clown pillow like a guillotine.

Grandpa made the best of being drafted, got his 21-gun salute at Arlington. But his dreams and nightmares were locked in his casket. Grandma's were locked in her poems of red roses and in her bottle-red hair. Her cheeks were soft as petals as she cooked the corn we shucked to Midwest perfection. At the table, no one talked of swords, just the weather and "Please pass the corn."

Grandpa was Sr. and my father was Jr. My father never went to war, except at home. When I was eight, we took a family trip to the Pacific, my favorite place to wash away his slurs and start fresh. The stiff wind breathed forgiveness. We parked on a cliff above the beach, and my toes ached to run through cold sand.

"Pass me my Jap Flaps," I said to my sister. She handed me the velvet and bamboo sandals from the back of the car. In bins at the store, bright signs called them Jap Flaps or Hong Kong Thongs. As the waves slammed the coast, my father's face turned purple.

"What did you call those?" he yelled from the driver's seat. Somehow, this anger was different than before, like the waves of the Pacific vs. Lake Erie's. As he pulled me from the car, the veins stood out on his head. The sandals in my hand fell to the sand.

His spanks never hurt much on the outside. But this time, his rage smelled like gunpowder. A strange metallic taste filled my mouth like blood on a sword. I felt disembodied, became the smiling clown head because I had to.

Now, decades later, I realize my father never liked that glass case either. Maybe he thought about the men who held the swords, their wives and daughters. Maybe he thought he was doing the right thing.

Standing above the Pacific where his father fought, Jr. tried to undo the crimes of Sr. by protecting my sandals from racial slurs. Maybe neither man was to blame for his rage, but instead, the legacy of patriarchy and of war.

The salt content of the world's oceans resembles that of human tears. But Jr. and Sr. never got to cry, all the world over. Instead, hands slapped and hearts closed. Wives and daughters cried, their soft petal cheeks folding with the years. Some wrote, and now we unfold the pages. The waves pound out a 21-gun salute over and over, as if to try again.

If the book is true, it will find an audience that is meant to read it.

Wally Lamb

.

A Brief History of

A Word with You Press:

Twelve years ago I was a jack of all trades, master of several, when an on-site job accident threw me into the briar patch, ("Oh, please, *pleeeeeeaaase,* Brer Fox, don't throw me into the briar patch!" Too late). Unable to ply my trade, I was forced to re-invent myself. I had written two books by then, and during my long and limited recovery had a chance to write a third, *The Boy with a Torn Hat.* For years preceding that, my link to the literary world had been to write book reviews for a leading newspaper, and that experience gave me an insider's view of publishing, which is forever the awkward intersection of art and business. I created *A Word with You Press* because I knew my chances of becoming published the year Random House laid off a hundred of its staff (recession, anyone?) had grown from dim to dark.

My website was conceived for the sole purpose of selling my novel, which eventually was nominated for Best Literary Fiction in 2010 by the USA Book Awards. But nobody just stumbles upon a website, so I advertised an online contest on Craigslist: Tell me a story, up to a page, about anything at all as long as you can tie it back to a cup of coffee, and I will publish the best one hundred in hard copy. The result was *The Coffeeshop Chronicles: Oh, the places I have Bean!* (I had over 500 inquiries and 150 entries).

The plan was that people would come to the site to read their contest entries posted, be charmed by *The Boy* welcoming them there, and buy me into the best-seller aisle in cyberspace.

I sold a staggering 20 copies this way. People were coming to see their *own* stories posted, read the comments other entrants had posted, and be on their way.

Except they weren't.

They kept coming back to enter fresh contests that offered prizes ranging from bizarre trophies that captured the theme of the contests, gift certs for

Starbucks or Red Lobster, Barnes and Noble, books, and even up to $500 cash.

And then, remarkably, we realized that we had not been nurturing a website, but a community of kindred spirits. I became as addicted as those the website seduced, looking forward to seeing the same writers returning and new ones coming for the first time with a story to tell.

Though we've expanded features (and countries!) to include more than just contests—over 50 since our inception in 2009—, contests remain the most colorful ribbon on the lure. We have hosted over a 150 workshops and meetups, published over twenty authors, been grant recipients from PEN USA to teach writing to children and have even hosted writing classes for children at our own facilities. Our highest profile event has become an annual tradition; a reunion of writers and artists at Rancho Villasenor each June in Oceanside, California, where everyone gets mic time to share their aspirations and accomplishments of the previous year, meet new people, and conspire to save the world.

Our website is whatever our visitors make of it, and we invite writers world-wide to enter our contests. We also provide award-winning editing and publishing services, detailed on our website, and have a standing offer to review up to thirty pages of your completed manuscript or work-in-progress without a fee to give you professional feedback.

Stop by for a cappuccino or a Budweiser (Ceske Budejovice produces 80,000 bottles an hour from the original, 14th century formula, not anything like your breakfast drink on the left side of the pond. I'm sure they won't miss a bottle or two.) And do visit our website and sign up for our feed at www.awordwithyoupress.com, and tell us about your project.

WAITING FOR MR. ED

Mike Stang

Trust me, I needed saving.

The time-portal-possibility I could've used to save myself, I slammed the door on—my past.

Forty-eight years later, I stood on the back porch of my grandfather's beach shack in a rage. My hands turned to fists and I beat the old screen door till it groaned away from a bottom hinge and swung like a crazy, hanging person. The place was deserted—one more along a shoreline developers knew was too far from the city to draw the millionaire's club; best just leave it to the periwinkles. I moved to a window and banged some more.

❧

There were four of us: my grandparents, Honey the dog, and me. We each pulled the other closer to the hearth in the winters when the bay froze and the pipes split. At night, Philco-neon characters stayed on till the storms cut the power. I kept one eye on the fence out front, if the snow buried it there'd be no school the next day. Times were raw, there was no money, but there was family.

I never thought when I turned my back on those two sweet people, I would want again so desperately what I so carelessly threw away. It was the cheap glitter I was after; it dragged me by the nose. I bragged about my creative personality, dreams full of imagination; the girls all wanting to talk to me. When I left Ma and Pa, I left my morals on their table.

"Mikey, wait," Pa said. I glared at him impatient; stupid. He reached into his pocket and pulled out some money. From another, this man who whispered me to sleep at night and lightly scratched my hands in the morning, drew a folded white handkerchief and gave it to me on top of the cash. My rebellion crumbled. I would've moved mountains to beg forgiveness and asked to stay, but it was time to go.

At first, I used his gift as a... as a handkerchief. I blew my nose in it but decided that wasn't right. I wrapped it around a small baggie of mushrooms. When I got to the desert I ate the mushrooms then used it as a bandana instead. I washed, cooked and cleaned with it. Used it as a tourniquet; everything.

Eventually, the holy rag, as my mind called it, claimed honor. It was no longer white, I no longer washed it. Stitched edging feathered like a war flag. I tied it around my neck and stuck out my thumb; a bit of right against a highway of wrong.

⌇

Almost half a century later the beach shack is overgrown in pines; a saddle-backed roof schemes with piano-fingered rot to bring it down. They are hereabout. I tell that to a patrol cop about to arrest me for trespassing. "Listen," I said. "I grew up in this shed, and those ghosts in there are my ghosts, and nothing will stop me from going inside. My business is with them."

⌇

Instinctively I used the handkerchief from my neck to wipe my forehead. Overwhelming memories carried me back to a night watching the snow. I didn't see the fence.

"Mikey?" My grandfather asked. "We'll shovel the paths clear tomorrow, all right with you?"

You bet it was.

Unless a reviewer has the courage to give you unqualified praise, I say ignore the bastard.

John Steinbeck

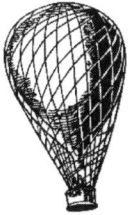

A SMALL, PRETTY HELL
(Fiction)

Kristy Webster

No one, not even you can convince me of the valley's beauty, especially in the Winter, especially in February when the snow is mostly gone, revealing the bald, dark patches of earth where grass should be.

You're still sleeping, or at least pretending to. You don't want another fight. I'm ready to head South, but you say we should wait it out a little longer. You say I'm panicked and hysterical. Really, I just don't like it here. Never did. Not when I was five and dad threw me in the backseat of his Plymouth or when mom pulled me out of school for a week because she was lonely without me. You think I should get over it. Only thing I'm getting over is you.

We've lived in our camper now for six months. The first three which were a Bohemian dream. The fourth month we had our first blowout fight where we both called each other asshole and stormed off, waiting for the other to run after us. The drama followed us into the fifth month, but now we're just tired, complacent. We don't make love anymore. I don't feel your fingertips running down my spine, grazing the back of my neck. I don't feel your warm breath. The cold is everywhere and everywhere.

I'm already dressed in layers, so I grab my beanie and some gloves. I climb out of the camper while you're still sleeping and the freezing air is like a snake around my neck, and the heat of my cigarette makes no promises. I take a deep, long drag before I look around at all the other RVs and motorhomes. Most people here are long termers. If some fancy mansion on wheels comes by, it's only for a night or two, only because of bad weather or poor planning. I hear hacking and spitting. Our neighbor chews tobacco.

Small mounds of dirty snow stubbornly cling to the little hillside behind the play area with a pained and rusted swing. I smell diesel because we're so close to the highway, and I feel the wolves in my belly awaken. The

Seabreeze convenience store carries Little Debbie's Snack Cakes and Diet Coke, the perfect breakfast for someone whose stopped caring. I know you'll shame me if you see me eating them, so I'll either have to eat a whole box or find a hiding place for what I can't finish. Your ex was a vegan and aspiring yoga instructor. I aspire for things too. I aspire to fill my empty belly with sugar and trans-fat, to have a moment where I feel bliss, even if I regret it minutes later. I aspire to find a reason to make it through the Winter in the same place I hated as a child, the place I swore I'd never return to. I aspire to find a purpose that will take me away from this father-mother shaped valley. So, when I see the toddler, her hair blonde and matted, wearing red, flannel pajamas running towards the highway, away from the campground, away from an invisible mother, I drop my smoke. I drop everything and run after her.

When I grab her, I immediately realize I've picked her up with too much force. She weighs as much as an empty paper bag. She's unbothered by the fact that I'm a stranger. Her eyes are wet and dead, and she smells like maple syrup and nicotine. Her boogers are frozen under her nostrils. Her fingers are turning purple, but she's not shaking. I continue to hold her up in front of me, assessing her. She's so limp and weightless, I watch her blink a few times to convince myself she's alive. Though I'd just seen her running seconds before, I'm not quite convinced she's breathing.

What's your name?

Where do you live?

Where's your mama?

Each question met not only with silence but apathy, until she points and grunts and says, "*daw, daw, daw,*" and I watch an emaciated German Shepard chewing on a meatless bone. She follows us, and I want so bad to pet her, show her some kindness, but then I remember the time my mother forced my hand, literally, told me that all dogs love all children. How I reached out to a mutt shivering outside of a 711. I remember the blood and the stitches. My energy must have scared the dog, mother said. I should learn to trust, she said.

I smile at the sad dog, I make a contract with my eyes.

Daw, the little girl says again, and finally, I place her on my hip and hold her like she belongs to me.

With my free hand, I search my coat pockets and find a scrunched up five-dollar bill and three quarters. I have enough for the snack cakes and a sixteen-ounce soda. When I walk into the convenience store with her, I feel her little fingers squeeze my arm and her cold cheek leans on my shoulder. I feel like I've grown a new part. The bell above the door rings, and the sad dog watches as the door swings closed. She'll be waiting.

I've never walked into any place with a child in my arms. When I was a kid this was a Mom and Pop grocer. They sold Nerds and Playboys. Now it's cell phone chargers, instant mocha machines, energy boosters, and the staples like beer and cigarettes. Baby girl starts bouncing on my hip, she starts grunting and pointing at food. It suddenly occurs to me, that I'm walking around with a stranger's child, and this is a small town full of small minds. This is a place that knows its children, for better or worse, who knows where they should and shouldn't be. But the man behind the counter is young, younger than you and I. He's scrolling on his phone, not watching us. He's given me the gift of invisibility. I stick a Slim Jim inside my coat and baby girl almost rats me out with her whining and begging, her reaching towards my coat. The young man looks up for a moment, clears his throat, then goes back to Tinder or Instagram or whatever it is that's fortunately kept his attention from us. I take one more chance and stick the bottle of soda inside my Carhart jacket, which is really your jacket. I go up to the counter with the Little Debbie's and a Lunchable I picked up for baby girl.

When I walk outside, Dog is already whining and wagging her tail. Baby Girl is working up to a scream, she's pulling at my coat and swinging her legs. Everybody wants something, I think. But not everybody needs as hard as these two do. I put Baby Girl down and tear the plastic off the Slim Jim before I hand it to Dog. Baby Girl cries out. *I know, I know.* I say. But I want to get her someplace warm first.

I don't want to wake you. Not because I'm being thoughtful, but because I don't want to share. So instead of going into the camper, I climb into the front cab of our truck. I sit Baby Girl down in the passenger seat and hand her the Lunchables. I finally pull out my soda and Little Debbie's snack cakes. Her dirty hands grab at the cheese and meat and she pushes them into her mouth. I hope she doesn't choke. I wouldn't know what to do. I turn the heat on full blast and the force of it blows some soft tendrils of yellow hair above her ears. She blinks, her eyes wet, her face a mess of crumbs and dirt now.

When I got pregnant you said it was up to me. I hated you for it. I still hate you for it. If my father were still alive, he would have told you it's not safe. He would have told you stories about falling in love with a wild woman. He would have explained that we don't just inherit eye color and straight hair, we inherit stories. He would have opened so many books, exposed chapters I want buried forever. My mother, if she were still alive, would tell you we should name our daughter after her mother, Patricia. My mother would have taken a quill to my womb, she would have made sure our child would come into the world wrapped inside her suffocating pages. You said it was up to me, so I did another hard thing without you.

The truth is, you're not as bad as all that. You dodge my blows. You love me when I'm unlovable. The truth is you want me to stay here for as long as it takes. You want me to look my devils in the eye. You won't touch me until I put out the fire beneath my skin. It's a mother and father and a baby I didn't have that burns me up so that I'm a walking pyre, searching for release.

Dog whines outside. She stands up on her back legs, pressing her paws up to the window. I think I could love her.

Daw, daw! Baby girl cries.

I take a piece of round turkey meat from her Lunchable and toss it to Dog. Dog catches it with her mouth. I wonder why no one is looking for Baby Girl or for Dog. I wonder what would happen if I took I tossed Baby Girl and Dog in the passenger cab and started driving, the way did when he took me and never brought me back.

Baby Girl looks sleepy now. I give her a sip of my Coke. I know that's bad for her teeth, but something tells me it's not the first time. I think how she hasn't cried out for her mama. Hasn't pushed me away. No one is calling for Baby Girl and no one is calling for Dog. I don't know why I do it, but I pick Baby Girl up, hold her tight, and whisper *I love you* into her ear. The stench of her is awful, layers of awful. But still I hold her tight.

By the time you wake up, she might be gone. Someone might finally realize their two-year-old is missing. Animal Control might come for Dog, lock her up until her time runs out. Or, by the time you wake, maybe I've named the dog, Our Dog. Maybe I've named the girl, Our Girl. For now, I'm dry heaving ghosts, pressing a strange child to my emptiness, ashamed of everything that I'm missing on the inside.

Your face appears to me in the passenger window. You're patting Dog's head and she's wildly licking your hand. Your face and the dog's face melt into one single question.

By the time you wake, I have lived life after life without you. I have motioned to the sky and to the earth to leave me here, to live in my own small, pretty hell.

HUMBLE BEGINNINGS

Ed Coonce

The floors were old wood, hewn from the scarlet oaks that grew nearby, and if you walked on them barefoot, you'd likely as not get a splinter or two. In the winter, when the sun darkened, and the snow fell silently outside, they would stoke the fire and curl up in blankets thrown on that rough floor and sleep. They held one another tight, sharing the same dreams. Those were the times when they had everything that they wanted, and all they wanted was each other.

She preferred sunny days and walks among the wildflowers, she would come home with blossoms in her hair and a song on her lips. Once, she brought home a little tabby who had been wandering in the woods. He took to her, and followed her everywhere. She often wondered about him, and what kind of person would desert a loving animal such as this.

He hewed things from wood and clay out in the small back lot, selling to the townspeople and furnished his home with handcrafted small comforts. They had no children, the sickness that had swept over them a few years earlier had left him and thousands of others unable to reproduce.

"You're shootin' blanks, Hank," the kindly country doctor told him.

The garden exploded in the summer months and they had the fresh food that sustained them. She canned and preserved, so that when the snows came, they could eat well. Once in a while they would drive their old sedan into town to pick up the mail, read the newspaper, catch a movie and stock up on things.

This chilly December day was different. They stopped outside the old general store for sugar and flour. She went in to shop, while he ran over to the news stand to pick up a copy of the Junction City Union.

JAPS BOMB PEARL HARBOR, the bold headlines read.

At their post office box there was another envelope, addressed to him and bearing the return address of the Selective Service Office.

Induction Notice, it said. He clutched the letter to his chest and hurried to the general store, where she was piling items into a bag.

She saw the stricken look on his face.

"Honey, what's wrong?"

"I have to go," he answered.

He showed her the draft notice. The tears came then, and for a while, they simply stood and held one another. "I love you," they told each other.

"Thank you," he told the store owner, who understood. His son had been called up earlier in the year. "God keep you safe," he told Hank Steffins, who had now been summoned to report for training, one of over three hundred thousand young men that year.

They spent Christmas Day preparing for his departure the next morning. She wiped her tears away and washed his socks and one set of clothes, spreading them out near the fireplace to dry. He stayed outside and chopped and gathered enough firewood to last her a good while. When her tasks were done, she prepared supper. They bowed their heads and prayed silently, and when the meal was finished, she drew him a warm bath.

While he soaked, she wrote him a letter.

"My dearest love," she wrote.

"I always, every minute of every day, want you so much. I will miss you awfully. Please write every chance you get, and please take care of yourself. This is a lock of my hair, it is all I have in this world to give you, and I hope that every time you hold this, you think of me and what we have together. I will be strong for you and will pray for you every day. Goodbye for now, my love.

Yours forever, Ruthie."

When finished, she put the letter and the brown curls in an envelope, sprinkled a few drops of perfume in, and sealed it up.

They spent their last night together, skin to skin, lips to lips, comforting each other.

The next morning he picked up his small bag and together, they drove to the train station, where several other young men were already standing, some with family, some without. The whistle of the approaching locomotive sounded in the distance. It would be there in a minute. They kissed one last time, and he left the car and walked to the platform. He looked around and waved.

Fighting back tears, she slid over into the driver's seat and put the old sedan in gear. It was up to the Almighty now, she thought. She remembered the envelope a half mile down the road. Panic-stricken, she turned the car around and raced back to the station. The last car was now a hundred yards down the tracks, picking up speed. The train was on its way and the love of her life was gone, heading off to war.

ONE WAY

Jon Tobias

Bud walks with the gait a tree might have had it suddenly grown feet. There is a certain joy to the movement as much as there is a fear that the next step is the one that plants him in his tracks. This movement is due to a pair of boots he purchased from a thrift shop that are too big for his feet. The brown boots with the Velcro straps aren't clown sized. They are just big enough to change the way he walks. That's how I see him now. I see him as a tree with just a few spots of blood on its roots.

As we come to a hill that turns into a sort of bridge that passes over a trolley crossing, he reaches out to hold my hand. I take it.

"If you fell down there it wouldn't kill you," I tease him.

"It would hurt."

"But you would survive," I say and lean over the edge. He responds by pulling me firmly back to his side.

"Being hurt is bad enough."

I hold his hand the rest of the hill.

"Where are we going."

"To visit a friend. You'll see."

"Okay. How come we didn't take your car?"

"It broke down. Remember?"

Cars speed by. The sound is relaxing like hard wind pulling rain into the sides of windows. I can fill my head with the angry hush of that sound. It is an exhausted father begging his children to sleep. To my thoughts, I say, "Shh. Please. Please. Please. Just shush."

"Now that I am old enough, can we have a beer when we get where we are going."

"A beer sounds nice."

A beer does sound nice. Sixty-five beers sound better. He lets go of my hand the way a child might drop something he is holding simply because he forgot he was holding it. Bud lumbers ahead of me a little swinging his arms in front of him. With the sun in my eyes and his big mop of curly hair bouncing, I think small tree. I think tall broccoli. He points to a gas station a few streets up and asks if we can go.

"When do you think we can go visit mom?"

"I'll call the hospital when we get to where we're going."

"Where are we going?"

"You'll see," I say less like it is a surprise and more like where we are going doesn't matter.

I think about his question about our mother. After seeing all that blood and the piece of glass sticking out of her cheek and lip like a walrus tusk, he still doesn't imagine the worst. Even with a second shard planted in her throat, he still thinks they can save her. Even after waiting with her for who knows how long for me to come and get him for our weekly day together, and after she stopped breathing, he still has hope. In his defense he didn't hear what the paramedics and police officer said. He didn't hear them say, "accidental death." Instead, before I made the 911 call, he heard me tell him to wait outside until I can get him.

"Can we get beers at the gas station?"

"Sure. Why not."

The door sensor chimes as we step inside. I tell him to pick something out and to grab a water for the rest of the walk. He chooses a six pack of spiked orange soda because all the other beers taste bad. He also chooses a refrigerated gallon of water.

The old cashier, who saw him choose the six pack, looks Bud up and down. It's not that Bud doesn't look his age, instead, it's that he sometimes gives himself away as someone with limited mental faculties. I prepare to give my speech about how it is his right to have a beer now and then, and how would he feel if someone told him he couldn't do what everyone else his age does just because he is a little different. I don't have to say anything. Bud places his ID on the counter and smiles. I pay. We leave.

Bud continues his lumbering walk, swinging the gallon of water back and forth like a cartoon mine worker with a pickaxe. I'm not sure if he recognizes where we are going yet, but I stop having to tell him left or right at different street corners. I wonder if it has crossed his mind yet that I'm going to leave him there.

"Do you think mom is going to haunt me if she dies?"

I tell him I don't know. I am glad to see the idea is finally working itself into his head.

"I was thinking, if she dies and haunts me then I can still see her. It will be like she never left. And because she's dead, if she calls me names like

116

she does when she's acting crazy, I can just put a cross in front of her face, and she'll disappear."

I tell him that would be nice I guess and that she'll always have to be kind to him if she wants to haunt him.

"If I die before you I promise to always haunt you, so you'll never have to be lonely."

We turn on to the street that Yvonne lives on. Her house is beige and perfectly plain. The front yard is pebbles and cacti instead of lawn. We walk up the freshly washed driveway, and I ring the doorbell. She answers.

"Hi, sis," I say.

"Hello? Hi Bud!" She tilts her head back and adjusts her glasses pretending she needs them to see him better. He laughs. She asks if it isn't my turn to spend time with him.

Bud waves even though he is a few feet away. "Hi Yvee, mom got drunk and died."

"Oh," she says, and, "Come inside."

I ask her where her husband, Mark is, and she replies that he's out of town.

"Why didn't you call? I could have picked you up."

"I needed the walk. We both did."

In the background I hear Bud pop the cap on his spiked soda and enthusiastically say, "Mmmmm. Spicy and refreshing." I look around the house. There are gold Klimt paintings on the wall, a spice rack with all the labels on the lids, pans hanging above the kitchen island, new furniture. From where I stand, I can see the freshly painted porch swing on the back patio. Here is where I tell her that I can't take him in, and that I need her to do it. Here is where she'll tell me that I need to quit trying to live my life as an artist and grow up.

"I need you to take him until I can find a job. A real job."

"I'm trying to start a family."

"Just until I can get out of renting rooms and into an apartment."

"It's not like I have a choice."

I shrug my shoulders.

"You can still create, but you need to grow up, selling art in coffee shops and on the street downtown won't make you a living," she says as she pulls a pan down from the rack. She then goes for bread from the cabinet followed by a block of cheese from the fridge.

Bud comes stumbling in from the living room. He stumbles from side to side with his shoulders hunched over. "Look. I'm mom," he says, and then falls into the wall knocking a painting to the floor. I have a moment of satisfaction at the painting falling because nothing I've made has been mounted on the walls of this house.

Bud apologizes and then stares at the painting with all of its gold swirls and spots of blacks and whites. He cries uncontrollably. He squats down over the painting and his tears and spit fall onto the canvas. He gets to his knees and starts clawing at it. The spiked soda lies on the light carpet next to him slowly forming an orange stain. I rush over to him and wrap my arms around him from behind pulling him against my chest and in between my legs.

"I pushed her," he says. The P sound forces a spray of saliva into the air. What lingers down his chin and onto my forearm. I think of palm fronds dripping dew.

"She fell through the porch window," I say.

"She's my only friend when you're gone, and she's mean."

"She fell."

"I yelled at her so hard that it knocked her down."

"You didn't do anything wrong, Bud. You can't push someone with your voice."

I rock him slowly and squeeze him hard. He hits me in the face with the back of his head and wiggles to escape my grip. I can already feel the blood pooling on my upper lip. I kiss the back of his head in the same spot where it connected with my nose and tell him I love him. He eventuallyrelaxes, letting his head fall back to my shoulder. He grabs my arm, and we sit like that for a while.

I tell him to put his beers in the fridge and to maybe lie down on the couch. Yvee tells him she'll bring him a grilled cheese and some water. He goes to the living room and turns on the television.

"Did you bring his medicine?"

"I just wanted to get us out of there. You didn't see it."

"Okay. We can go back for some of his stuff, and I'll take you to your place."

We eat in silence. We wake Bud, who is asleep on the couch, and tell him we'll be back. He falls back asleep almost immediately. Yvee starts the car, and the back up camera comes on. I can see our dirty footprints across the driveway on the screen. One set is much larger and more visible as if someone painted them on. The other set is barely there.

"You can live at mom's house with Bud," Yvee says.

"You should sell it. I can't live there. Not after everything."

"What are you going to do?"

"I, uh, I'll start looking for a real job, and he can live with me when I get an apartment of my own."

"I'm just trying to start a family of my own."

"I know."

"I'll call the hospital when I get home and take care of things," she says before turning the radio on.

The drive feels long, and the sunset which would normally inspire me to paint, instead feels like the last thing a bug smashed against a windshield sees before the wipers fling its carcass to the wind. As I get out of the car, Yvee hands me a fifty and says she loves me. I tell her I love her too, and she drives off.

I am not ready to go upstairs yet. I'm not ready to go back into my tiny bedroom packed with shitty art. I'm not ready to hop on my laptop and start looking for work. I'm not ready to say, "Debit or credit," to lines of people who think my only job is to say, "Debit or credit." I love Bud, but I'm not ready to be our mother.

Instead of going up, I turn right and walk longer. My feet feel like paint cans full of cement. My heart feels like a man hanging by the branches of my ribcage. I stop at the greyhound station. I sit inside long enough that most of the people inside aren't going anywhere but are instead looking for a warm place to rest. A security guard to harasses me along with most of the others about being there. The screen hanging above the automated ticket booths shows the next bus is going to Texas. I slide the fifty Yvee gave me into one of the machines and tap the button that says, "One Way." I'm sorry, Bud. I'm not ready.

*Good fiction's job is to comfort the disturbed
and disturb the comfortable.*

David Foster Wallace

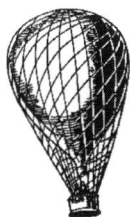

THE SECRET

Mike Stang

Jack was late as usual. He never seemed to be able to master the cycle of late night boozing, getting little to no sleep, then dragging his sorry butt out the door the next morning. But today—of all the days to be late—today was surf finals. What was he thinking?

Betty was thinking the same thing. She's put up with a lot from her husband over the past three years. Jack's rise up through the ranks to top contender was a Cinderella story: natural talent and a love affair with the ocean made quick work of the competition. Those days at every surf spot Jack pulled into fans waited on him. It was crazy. Along the beaches and in the local bars, the talk about Jack was a sure thing. Everyone cheered: bikini-clad girls giggled at him, a sales rep had a wax named after him and magazine photographers arrived whenever Jack paddled out—uninvited. Things were looking good; real money just around the corner.

Betty saw it differently. She knew Jack wouldn't see it through, fifteen years of marriage said so. Oh he'd get all excited with the best of them: feel proud, non-stop right through to the confident stage, slip up then come back stronger; all the stuff you saw in the movies, but Betty knew he would reach a point and walk away.

～

"Jack's never had fame nor money for that matter. I won't pin it all on him when the time comes."

"You will, and he'll be worse off for it, but that's your business, he's your husband, all you been through with this shit. Ever talk to him about carpentry anymore?"

"Until he threatens to hit me. One of these nights he just might, but I don't think so."

"Yeah, Jack's a drunk but he ain't mean."

"Shut-up. You got no right to say that."

"Whatever, I just mea ..."

"Who the fuck do you think you are? He's my Jack, y-you go to hell."

Betty threw the phone on the bed next to her. She picked up the habit from watching tv soaps at night; all the rage—go-to response for emotional emergency. What else was she going to do? Jack wasn't there to yell at. He was never there anymore: down at the Surf bar talking about the day's point break with whoever would listen—they all listened, or over at Harry's shop in the back, shaping boards. Two or three in the morning she would see him come to bed. She'd look at him once to make sure he wasn't bleeding then give him her back.

~

The kayak banged around in the back of Jack's truck covered in seaweed and mud left over from yesterday's afternoon set. Running the rocks along the coast ahead of a double overhead is about as thrilling as it gets around here, except when the storms come in the winter. Then it's balls to the walls. Sixteen to twenty-four foot combers lined up on the horizon. There's no sense in timing them, just get out there and get your ass kicked and hope you can stay on the ride long enough to get dumped close to the beach.

Well, it was winter, and there was a storm, and it was the same kind of lunacy the surf gods decided to give the day of the finals. Jack stopped the truck and looked out at the water. The storm pushed enough water under the waves to make them heavy and slow with tremendous power. He felt the earth shake when they gave up their curl and crashed on the beach. Smaller breakers came in at different directions and climbed the backs in between the monsters. They were lighter and faster and cascaded down twenty-foot faces. The sea was nothing but a giant washing machine. He wondered, along with a growing sense of dread, why the contest hadn't been cancelled.

This is fucked up, Jack told himself. He wasn't so full of himself not to respect the nature of the beast. Fear trolled the bottom of his stomach. It was good strategy to wait until the last heat, maybe the sea would settle down by then. It didn't work. The wind changed to on-shore and stiffened.

Three surfers waited on the horn, edged up to the shore with a grip on their kayaks; six knees knocked each time a wave came in: Harry, as experienced a surfer as Jack, Roy, the new comer to town barely sixteen years old, and Jack, the incumbent owner two years running of the crown.

Harry turned to Jack's ear and had to scream to be heard over the Banshee pandemonium. "What, do, you, think?"

"We can call this off if you want to. Already sent two surfers earlier to the hospital."

"WHAT?" Harry screamed louder.

"Not. Worth. It!"

Roy started to shake uncontrollably. His eyes bulged. The sight of the overheads towered over him and welded his body to the spot. Harry reached over with his free hand and pulled Roy's head to him until their foreheads touched.

"Get out of here," he mouthed to the kid, slow, then squeezed Roy's neck to tell him there was no shame. Not today. Roy turned to go when the horn went off. Jack couldn't believe the sponsors expected the competition to continue and it pissed him off. All three surfers turned up the beach and flipped a finger towards the tents. Other surfers grabbed the horns and threw them in the dunes; couple of tables flipped over but Jack couldn't really tell what was going on.

Roy suddenly appeared by Jack's side and locked foreheads. "We gonna do this or what?"

Jack knew the kid wouldn't quit unless he did. *I give him that,* Jack thought. He also knew Roy wasn't strong enough to handle the murderous undercurrents. If he got hurt or worse Jack would forever hold himself responsible. *I can't do that to you,* Jack told himself as he looked directly into Roy's eyes. "I'm going to the bar. Wanna come?"

Roy nodded and broke away.

The trio headed back towards where the trucks were parked, leaving fin trails, which instantly disappeared under miniature tsunamis. Harry took off right away, disgusted. Jack was about to get out of his wetsuit when he noticed Roy was missing.

Damn it, he was right behind me. Jack looked back at the beach and saw the last of Roy's kayak enter the water. *Oh shit, oh shit no;* Jack sprinted. He couldn't be late for this.

~

"Not that you deserve it, you hear about your Jack?"

"You got some nerve calling here."

"Pulled that kid Roy out of the sea. Saved his life they say. Go see him at the hospital if you want."

"Who? The kid?"

"Jack."

~

A haggard nurse walked up to Betty in the hall. *Fourth one today,* she mumbled to herself. "Ma'm, Jack is coming out of surgery now, if you could just wait a bit." She held out her arms like a traffic cop.

Betty ghosted her and found Jack's room on the third floor. He looked peaceful with his eyes closed. The right shoulder was mummy-wrapped and both knees hung from straps. She took a hand in hers and bent to kiss the lone clear spot left on his face.

"Jack," she whispered. "Honey, you okay?"

His eyes uttered open and found his wife right away. He squeezed back where she held him.

"Roy," he asked.

"He's in good shape, Jack. The EMTs were in time."

"How about you, baby, how's your shape doing." Her husband ran his hands up her arms.

"Jack! It's those drugs they gave you."

"Give me a few hours." Jack failed at winking. "I'm gonna open the shop again, you know."

"Which one?"

"The one with all the carpentry tools. Gonna need your help, wife. Ready to put your belt back on?"

"Hurry home, babe."

～

Betty took the back stairs exit but bumped into a bikini girl wrapped in a blanket, sipping on something over by the loading dock.

"You're Betty, right, Jack's wife? Do you even know what a hero Jack is?"

"I'm getting the idea."

"Oh, my, god he ran into that surf and pulled Roy out bare handed. I've never seen anything like that except on tv then ..."

"Take a breath, girl. Slow down."

"Right—whoo—then a wave crashed on top of them and Jack shielded Roy with his body it was so cool ..."

Betty kept walking to her car. She left the girl talking through a rolled-up window.

The shop was still there. *Under several layers of dust,* she reminded herself. *That's okay, the dust will find the tv instead.*

～

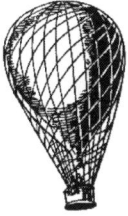

A YOUNG WIFE'S TALE
(Non-fiction)

Kristy Webster

You become a mother a month before your twentieth birthday. Before that you were a child scolded for raising her shirt above her nipple, for pressing the plastic mouth of a baby-doll to her chest and mimicking what she'd seen the dark-skinned women of your church practice openly. Your mother in turn, put tiny bottles in your hands—one painted white, the other painted orange. This meant the little skirt of your blouse rested on the elastic waist of your pants. This meant you obeyed not your instinct but the voice of your mother who cooked you rice with runny yoked eggs for lunch.

You were nineteen-years-old and your son only two days young when your milk came in, filling up your breasts mercilessly. Choking on tears, you raced to the bathroom, to the light, to the mirror. You unbuttoned your floral pink nightgown, a gift from your mother-in-law, and looked at yourself. *These were not your breasts. This was not your body.* This was your son's mother's body. You were nineteen and slight and just a little wounded, but this was not your body: a body on fire, lava milk engorging what were once your small, apricot breasts. You wailed. Your husband who groggily wiped sleep from his eyes was shocked into full consciousness not by your cries but by the sight of your new animal body. *Honey,* he whispered, *oh god honey...*

You hadn't yet lowered your arms to your sides. You held them at an angle, bent at the elbow, afraid to touch this foreign body, your nightgown in a pool of cotton fabric at your feet. You watched white droplets blossom from your bulging, stretched out brown nipples. Slowly you lowered both arms to your side and noticed this enticed a steady stream of white molten, you pressed your arms tightly to your body, to the side of your breasts until the pressure caused your breasts to burst with milk, splattering the mirror in front of you. You gasped and bawled until you heard the faintest giggle, your husband trying to muffle his laughter. Your tears turned to laughter, too, not right away, but soon enough. You'd named your son Isaac, Isaac which means laughter.

When the baby woke, you pressed your full breast into his tiny pink mouth, and the milk expressed with such force you thought he might drown in it, but he drank as if he were something supernatural, an Uber Being: Son with Mythical Thirst.

Your son's tiny fingernail caught on your areola as he drained your breasts of both milk and pain. His eyes rolled inside the back of his head like a drunken little man, and you knew that this was still your body, but now it was also a body built for him. Your tears ghosted away while that blue-white nectar left your body, left your breasts supple and light once again. *Girl, there you are, there you are girl.* And the baby boy? He is panacea and hero, both an angel and a vampire.

~

Before he left you for a younger girl—you were the oldest twenty-four-year-old alive—he took you to see Shakespeare in Ashland, Oregon. Over a bowl of lobster ravioli, you would talk details; he would move out, you would stay in the house with the boys. He would pay the mortgage in lieu of child support. An olive-skinned waitress with bluish green eyes and dark hair, much like you but far taller, walked with purpose between round tables and hot dishes, legs half extended into aisles. While the impending separation floated in the steam of the hot pasta, you wondered if maybe it had something to do with beauty. You saw yourself in the waitress's features. But she attended her guests half-cocked and half-interested, her hair longer and lighter than yours, her vagina perhaps narrower, or tighter and perhaps she was well-traveled, perhaps she was made more beautiful by all the things you'd lost, or you never had.

You continued to eat well between plays. You fantasized about starting your new life as a single mother living in this magical place, imagined being a girl with a past turned to sand. You imagined your boys, aged one and four: the firstborn, a chestnut-haired warrior, the second born, a bald-headed Buddha living in a one-bedroom apartment. You'd maybe take up acting. You'd maybe fall in love with a Hamlet or an Othello, god forbid, a Romeo. You'd wait tables, and maybe one night, you'd see yourself in the face of a girl like you, a girl whose paper world had burned up in the candlelight in the wake of dinner rush, in the chaos of tourist season between *Much Ado About Nothing* and just plain nothing.

What had he said in the car, on the drive down from the Olympic Peninsula? He had said he loved you still, maybe, but he was no longer in love with you. You were not sure if the anger in his voice was directed at you, at himself or at something else entirely. If so, what could be the "something else entirely"?

Your second day in Ashland the sun is shining on your five foot five 135lb frame, your buttoned-down white lace blouse and your black workpants. You and your husband are playing your last game of house. He takes your picture sitting in front of a fountain and you're smiling for the game and for the day, because you are not entirely heartbroken, not yet. Your hair is rippled with tiny waves from taking out the corn rows your best friend had braided; braids for a girl not entirely white, for a girl not entirely "girl" or woman but an in between thing, plus this: a mother.

In the park he takes another picture of you. You've removed your white lace blouse, shed down to your sleeveless black tank, your arms exposed. This time you're not looking at the camera, but at the ducks in the lake. You're smiling. You're a winner at this game.

When you take a seat at a picnic bench, a large splinter stabs through your work pants, into the meatiest part of your thigh right below your right butt cheek. You pull out what you can, the pain surprising you because the day is too beautiful for pain, and though you knew your heart had reason to feel heaviness, your heart chose lightness. Now, the pain demanded you felt what needed to be felt in a different part of your body.

Halfway through Henry the VIII, you tell your husband the pain is unbearable. That night in the bed and breakfast he tries to help you pull more of the splinter out, but the skin has sealed it in. You take the tweezers into your own hand and try to dig out the culprit. The more you dig, the more the splinter falls apart into tiny pieces, covered in mucous and blood. The pain is outstanding, and you feel it surging down your leg. You feel it in other places it shouldn't exist, too, like your hands, your lungs, your neck.

You put ice on your bottom and try to fall asleep. It's your last night in Ashland. It's your last night with your husband, too. The moon and the splinter won't let you sleep. You turn to your husband, disrobe, and climb on top of him. You tell him, *Just one more time.* He calls you by your name, not honey, or sweetie, or baby, but the name your parents gave you when you were born into this world. He says, *Please, no.* You say, *Please, yes, one last time.* You cry as you rock your hips back and forth, he cries a little too. You cry not because you feel the sting of the splinter embedded in your flesh with every thrust, but because this was how you made your sons and your sons belong to you both, but you know that soon they will belong to you even more.

～

The first thing you do is beg him to take the bed and he does. It's a cherry finish sled bed frame, queen-size. You have no need for a queen because now you will be sleeping alone. You replace it with a twin-sized bed and you replace colorful bedding with a white eyelet bedspread and sheets.

The first night is a relief. Every night after that is a hell you can't sleep through.

Your older son has fits, and though he's had fits before, these fits are intended to remind you that a dagger has been thrown into the middle of his heart. He screams at you, not because he's tired or jealous of his cherub-faced baby brother, but because his world has split in two and he's four and he knows nothing will ever be the same, but he also knows nothing. He doesn't realize that at twenty-four, you know only a little more than he does, and you feel his tantrums in your womb where he used to live, and his anger in your breasts where he used to feed. You feel the phantom pain of milk weighing them down, changing their shape. He cries, *You made my daddy go away!* Sometimes, you think maybe he is right. Maybe you did. Maybe it was your low sex drive. Maybe it was because of how deeply you fell in love with your babies, how the creating and growing of life, then sustaining it with your own body satisfied or overwhelmed any need for intimacy, leaving little if anything for your husband. Maybe. Still, the little house you painted yellow, the little house you were going to grow old in, has turned into a battlefield and your armor and artillery have turned to soot.

‿

A year later, after being released from an eight-day psychiatric hold following a half-cocked suicide attempt, you drive away from the devastating heat of the Yakima Valley with your newly released hospital roommate, Vicki. Vicki drives you to the little Victorian Seaport on the Olympic Peninsula, to the house you'd once shared with your husband, your two sons and a puppy named Nina. Before you have a chance to knock on the door a yellow-haired girl with an eyebrow ring stands in the doorway of what was once your home, holding your blue-eyed, blonde-haired son in her arms. Your baby is stroking the girl's pony-tail with one hand, holding an orange Popsicle to his little mouth with the other. The irony that he resembles the girl more than he does you doesn't escape your notice. It doesn't matter if he drips orange Popsicle juice all over your clothes, it doesn't matter if his diaper stinks. You only want to put his skin to your skin. You wonder how you ever thought you could leave this world when part, if not most of you, still drums inside the hearts of your sons.

She gives you a tour of your own house, highlights the changes made, but all you want is your son back in your arms. She complains about a set of dishes, asks you to take them with you, they're not her style. You recognize the China pattern. They were a wedding gift from your former mother-in-law. The yellow-haired girl tells you she's sorry she lied to you last summer. She knew all along that he was married.

Your older son is the first to return to you. He walks over to you and

128

you kneel to face him. You put your arms around him and hold him tight. You remember the flowers their father sent you while you were in the hospital, the note attached that said, "You are Isaac's entire world. Please, don't ever do this again."

Though you're overmedicated on 900 milligrams of Neurontin which weakens your courage and dampens your response time, you finally reach out to your baby, the one in the diaper and t-shirt, the one with the sticky fingers. He may not look like you yet; he doesn't have your dark hair, your olive skin, but he still fits on your hip like he did before, he still melts into your shoulder, the curve of your neck.

The girl takes you up the stairs to show you what "they've" done to the bedrooms. Her clothing fills each closet in every room of your former house. She hands you a green skirt, hemmed with bright, colorful orange, red and yellow beads, tells you it's much too large on her, it will fit you, she says. Later that afternoon, Vicki will tell you that she'll kill the bitch for that alone.

When you leave the house, queasy, slightly numb, the nineteen-year-old girl stands on the porch and waves goodbye. Vicki's face is redder, her eyes greener than before. She stares at you expectantly, waiting for your colors to deepen, for the steam, the smolder. But the smell of your child's skin and hair, the sight of your five-year-old's small red pout, wash over you, casting a cool, pale light. You look back at that grenade of a girl, that yellow-haired catalyst, and rather than go to war, you thank her. You thank her for the skirt, but really, you're thanking her for blowing up your former world, your former life. You thank her because your dream window has widened, and your path is glowing before you. You thank her because your steps are feeding invisible embers, you're on fire but you don't burn.

THE LAST NUMBER

Laura Elizabeth

As parents, we're told we must give while expecting nothing in return, since children think only of themselves. But the opposite is true. My daughter's first word was "Duboo" (Love you). The night before her birth, her silvery voice rose in a dream from the amniotic oceans, "I want to be borned, Mama."

At two, she recalled that time, "When I was in your tummy, it was cozy and your heart go boom-boom." She'd grab my face and blurt, "You're not Mama, you're You!" acknowledging my humanity separate from my role. Nursing, she'd ask politely, "Two, please!" Later she became more brazen, figured out the math for more: "Four, please!"

She'd ask unabashedly for what she wanted, but with a compassion akin to Ghandi. When I sighed with tiredness, she'd run to me in Minnie Mouse PJs, further delaying my trip to the bathroom. She'd embrace my legs, cooing, "You're being very patient. You're my good sport." She gave me back the words I gave her every day. "Mama, you're my special daughter," she whispered as she caressed my calves. I was awed as by first snow.

At three, when asked what she wanted for Christmas, she outlined her career goals: "I want to drive a bulldozer and I want to be an elf." But she knew those were only wants. She only needed one thing: "I really need a moose!" She woke easy to the enormous gift of a day. "It's a day today!" she'd holler as the sun rose. This is how she prayed. I wish I could be as good at it.

At four, she invited me into her ladybug tent, the thin red walls a barrier between childhood and adulthood. "Stop what you're doing and do some important work. Come. Play." With sticky fingers, she handed me her Etch-a-Sketch.

At five, she had love emergencies worthy of a cop visit. Skipping down the sidewalk, she'd scream, "I love you so much I can't stand it! I love you with Joy! I love you Way Bad!"

Now, at six, she considers important questions. "What comes after the sky? What comes after the last number? Because I love you more than that." We have love contests to see who can express it more. "I love you more than you! I love you more than love!" The only two that are impossible. "Heck the what?" she laughs.

This is the math of life. "I love you a google, a billion percent, "she says, squinting at the limits of language. Finally, she has it. "I love you more than Italy, Saturn, and cheetahs!"

So this is for you, little one. I vow to get down on the rug and play mermaids till we're old, even if I'm late to work. I love you more than fear. And I love you more than Italy, Saturn and cheetahs.

In fact, I'll take you to Italy, help you save the cheetahs, show you Saturn through a telescope. And I love you as much as, but not more than, words. Because with these words, we build that love.

Author Mischka Blank (*The Seven Bridges of Prague*) visiting the Towers that are *A Word with You Press* in České Budějovice

(Condensed and modified from the article as published in Legacy Arts Magazine)

Recently I bellied up to a bar in Bohemia that smelled of Hemingway. The bartender, a somewhat evasive Honduran, confessed upon hearing I was a publisher that he kept a journal (after the gratuitous I'm not a writer, but...).

We bargained: an opinion on his first three pages in exchange for a rum and coke. I prepared myself, given the circumstances, to be under-whelmed. Instead, I discovered prose that would make a vineyard weep wine. The first of almost 1,000 pages documenting an adventure and a truly impossible love story.

"What is this?"

"It's about me and Emma. We walked across Africa together." He told me more, much more. A love story that endured until it didn't, but he could never forget her.

"What do you want to see happen with this?"

"I want a book out of it."

"Of course." Isn't that what every writer tells me?

But he continued. "Just one book."

"Just one?"

"Yes. To give to Emma. So she will know I loved her."

What finer motive can there be to writing your story—be it novel or memoir—than to present it to the ones you love to authenticate what you feel for them, or what's inside your head and heart? It certainly trumps writing for fame or fortune.

Isn't your life a novel, really? Not an aimless meandering, but something with purpose and value? You are the central character, and you have been faced with obstacles along the way. Did they beat you down? Did you overcome them?

The *5x5* authors, keeping this dream aloft, all defied gravity, a law meant to be broken. Are you pondering breaking the law and joining them? Maybe this from Steven Pressfield will help:

When we conceive an enterprise and commit to it in the face of our fears, something wonderful happens. A crack appears in the membrane.

Like the first craze when a chick pecks at the inside of its shell. Angel midwives congregate around us; they assist as we give birth to ourselves, to that person we were born to be, to the one whose destiny was encoded in our soul, our daimon, our genius.

Or, as Goethe said:

Whatever you can do, or dream you can, begin it. Boldness has genius, magic, and power in it. Begin it now.

Goethe's editor at Nike thought even that a little too wordy:

Just do it!

We are all conformists, but the difference between people is whether it is to their fears or their desires that they conform.

Thornton Sully

The Editor-in-Chief at home in the Czech Republic, willing to edit everything – except his own desires..

STAFF AND ASSOCIATES

Thornton Sully,
Editor-in-Disbelief

Thorn has Jack-Londoned his way across the globe sleeping with whatever country would have him, and picking up stray stories along with way. A litter of dog-eared passports that have taken up residence in his sock drawer are a constant temptation, but, as the founder in 2009 of A Word with You Press, dedicated to helping you tell your story persuasively and with passion, it's not likely he will stray too long from the Towers that are A Word with You Press in historic České Budějovice in the Czech Republic, where he lives with the love of his life having the time of his life.

I arise in the morning torn between a desire to improve the world and a desire to enjoy the world. This makes it hard to plan the day."

Thornton Sully, plagiarizing E.B. White

Tiffany V,
Contributing Editor

With a master's degree in Transformative Language Arts, plus TLA membership and certification, Tiffany is a joyful TLA practitioner. She loves being an Associate Editor for *A Word with You Press*, too. Her favorite genres to edit are poetry, young adult, science fiction, fantasy, and thrillers (bring on the horror, it doesn't scare her). Tiffany's an avid reader, with an eye for comprehensive editing. In her first book of poetry, *Ugly Drawers, Pretty Panties*, Tiffany shares intriguing verbal vignettes. Currently, she is honored to lead as President of the San Diego Book Awards. She's also a San Diego Kingdom Writers Association Vision Lead, a member of ASCAP, The National Forensics League, and involved with the Transformative Language Arts Network magazine, Chrysalis. Tiffany is the quintessential Renaissance Gal.

Stefanie Allison,
Associate Editor

Stefanie Allison has been involved with *A Word with You Press* since 2010 and has since become an associate editor. She currently has three novels-in-progress, two of which were NaNoWriMo winners for 2017 and 2018. She currently resides in Los Angeles, California.

Kristine Starr,
Associate Editor

Kristine is an energetic New Yorker who learned everything she knows by getting beat up in NYC public schools. Fighting her way from the canyons of Queens College through Columbia University, she cut her teeth on Capitol Hill. After leaving politics, she worked various freelance editing and teaching gigs. This led to the establishment of her education company which creates custom curriculum for learners outside of a traditional school environment.

Derek Thompson,
Associate and Contributing Editor

I've been part of the *A Word with You Press* family since 2010 after a fortuitous virtual encounter with Thorn. I'm a former Londoner, released into the wild many years ago. I write fiction, non-fiction and comedy material. My backlist includes: a series of British spy thrillers (intrigue, action, and sardonic humour – with a nod to Raymond Chandler and Len Deighton!); a magical fantasy novel; a children's story about bullying and transformation; a whole bunch of gags for performance, radio and greetings cards; a few short stories that appear in obscure anthologies, a very short film script, and a feature for The Guardian. None of these make me a writer. That title is bestowed on *anyone* who dares pick up a pen and puts their truth (real or imagined) on the page.

Find him online at: *amazon.com/Derek-Thompson/e/B0034ORY08* or *twitter.com/DerekWriteLines*

Teri Rider,
Book Designer

"I love to work with authors to build beautiful books. My profession has intertwined art and design for over three decades and after trying many things, I've landed in the lap of my favorite: All things books. Find me at *TopReadsPublishing@gmail.com.*"

Aren Ock,
Book Designer

Aren is a freelance subeditor specializing in ESOL and academic arts texts. They received a Bachelor of Arts with first class honours in English literature and creative writing from the University of Kent, then spent a few years in copy writing and media insight. Aren leapt into the arts and smarts in 2014, enjoying diverse experience in academia, visual and performance art and film production, editing, publishing, and poetry. Aren lived, studied, and worked in Prague for several years, where they led Thorn by the nose through the Prague literary scene. Aren now lives on a boat on a river in London: the kind of conventionality typical of all our staff.

Ben Angel,
Associate Editor

With 42 countries and four continents under his shoes, Ben M. Angel has traveled a bit from his Northwestern US roots... in fact, three times around the world (twice eastward, once westward). Despite (or perhaps because of) this, he has a fascination with history and its effect on the interconnectedness of people around the globe. He is an active member of the Wrocław, Poland, Internations community and a co-Consul of its Writers' Kaffeeklatsch, as well as a Volunteer Curator on the Geni.com social networking genealogical website. He previously served as Editor-in-Chief of a student newspaper, production manager at a small English-language news agency based in mid-1990s Kyiv, Ukraine, geotechnical engineer-in-training in Alaska, Washington State, and New Mexico, environmental consultant in Azerbaijan and Qatar, FEMA contractor in Alabama, and a Philippino construction company management consultant in the. Nevertheless, he persists in writing, these days mostly as an English-language freelancer based in Eastern Europe, where he raises alongside his native Belarusian wife a daughter and a son.

David Wogahn,

Affiliate and Contributor

David Wogahn is the president of AuthorImprints, an award-winning, professional self-publishing services company. He has helped more than 100 authors, businesses and other organizations launch self-publishing imprints which, in turn, has resulted in the successful publication of more than 300 books and counting...

www.authorimprints.com/about

Laura A. Roser,
Affiliate and Contributor

Laura Roser is the Founder and CEO of Paragon Road, the leading meaning legacy planning company. She's also the Amazon #1 bestselling author of *Your Meaning Legacy: How to Cultivate & Pass On Non-Financial Assets.*

Her work focuses on helping individuals create a legacy of excellence — from philanthropic strategies to family legacy planning to the creation of creative collateral.

She is the editor in chief of *Legacy Arts* magazine and has interviewed many top CEOs, high net worth individuals, spiritual leaders, philosophers, financial professionals, family experts, celebrities, philanthropists, and innovators to uncover how to craft a more meaningful life experience. She has written articles about legacy planning for financial publications such as ThinkAdvisor, Iris.xyz, and *Kiplinger.*

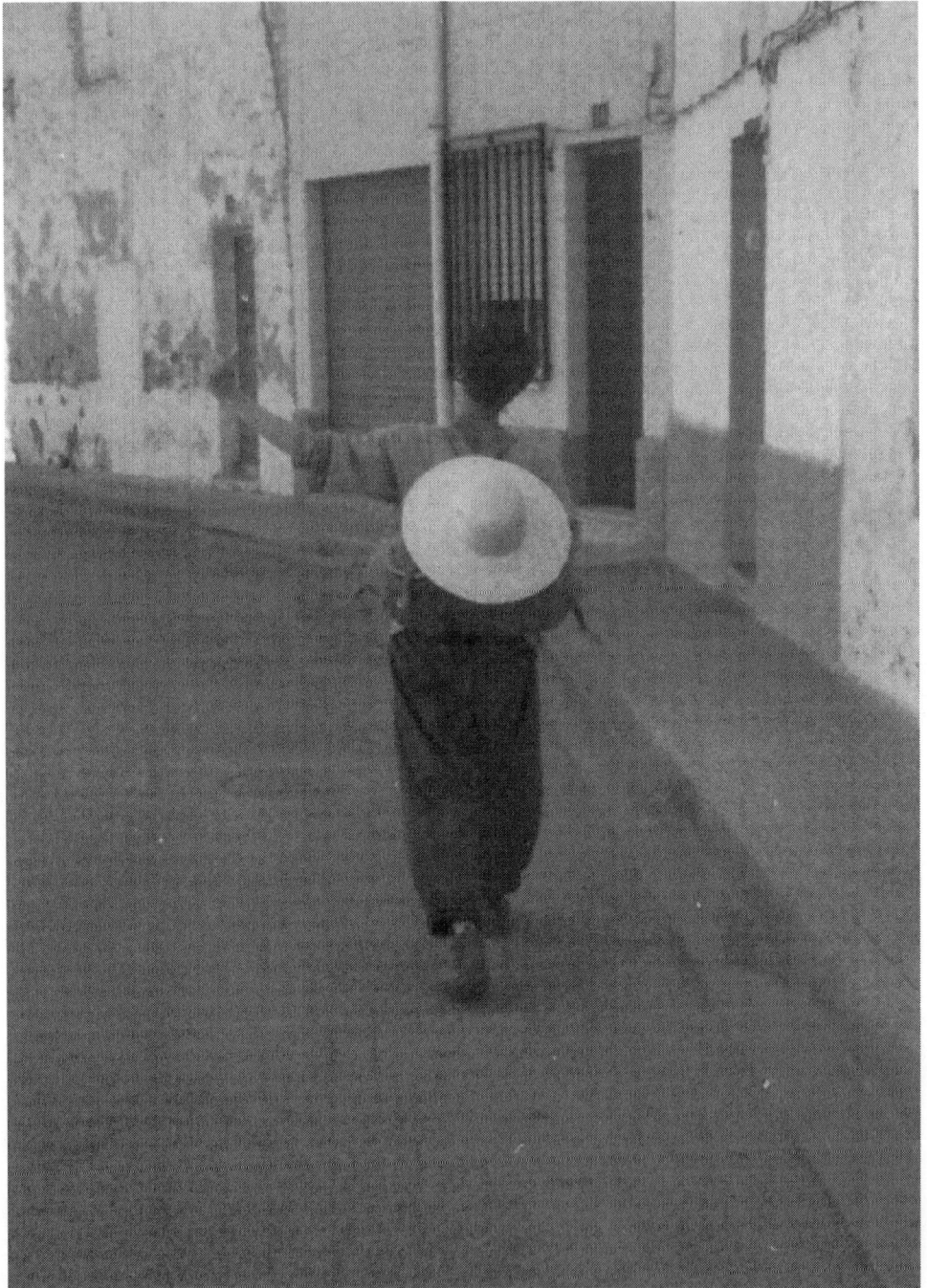

Join us on the Great Adventure!

A word about

A Word with You Press

We are a playful, passionate, and prolific consortium of writers connected by our shared love of the written word.

Are you drawn to the notion that there is nothing more beautiful or powerful than a well-told story? We are.

For a decade, A Word with You Press has been helping storytellers to become writers, and writers to become authors.

Our secret knowledge, revealed:

A writer is among the lucky few who discovers that art is not a diversion or distraction from everyday life; rather, art is an essential expression of the human spirit.

Monika Spykerman
former Associate Editor, *A WwYP*

Writing is a pleasure, and we are here to amplify the joy it brings to the writer and the reader. That is our mission. Do you have something to say? We'd like a word *from* you.

Thorn,

Editor-in-Chief, tour guide
thorn@awordwithyoupress.com

A Word with You Press
Editors and Advocates for Fine Stories in the Digital Age
With Offices and Affiliates in the USA, the UK, Germany, Poland, and the Czech Republic
www.awordwithyoupress.com

PATRONS

We'd like to thank the following patrons who helped to keep the dream aloft (and thanks to those of you who donated after this went to print):

Kristine Grant
Relationshift: The Right Words for What You Really Want to Say
www.inspiredheartletters.com

Mike Casper
The Sing Song Child: A Love Story
thesingsongchild.com
Stone Thrower
www.mcasper.com

Laura Roser
Your Meaning Legacy: How to Cultivate & Pass On Non-Financial Assets
Legacy Arts Magazine
www.ParagonRoad.com

Stefanie Allison
Lightning in the Oak
Spirit
Witness
www.paranormalauthoress703.wordpress.com

Mike Stang

Gabriella Jones

Roxanne Kane

Diane Pipkin

Lori Celaya
Nos pasamos de la raya/We Crossed the Line
www.thriftbooks.com

Lisa Johnson

Lynn Buettner
https://lynn-buettner.pixels.com/

Daniel Hare

Austin Storm

F.J. Dagg

The Lowlands of Heaven
Branch 92 Publications

David Wogahn
*Register Your Book: The Essential Guide to ISBNs, Barcodes, Copyright,
and LCCNs*
*Successful eBook Publishing: The Complete How-to Guide for Creating
and Launching Your Amazon Kindle eBook*
www.davidwogahn.com

Kimberley Cudahy

Nina Valentina

Stan Katz
The Emperor and the Spy
The Art of Peace: The Illustrated Biography of Prince Tokugawa
www.theemperorandthespy.com
theartofpeacebiography@gmail.com

Jeanette Thornton

Sally Pla
The Someday Birds
Stanley will Probably be Fine
Benji, the Bad Day, and Me
www.sallyjpla.com

Tiffany Vakilian
*Ugly Drawers, Pretty Panties: A Collection of Poetry, Prose, Dreams and
Missives*
www.tiffanyvakilian.com

Thanks for the gift of flight!

The rest of this page was intentionally left blank. Find a quill. Write the first sentence to *your* story. It may never be finished, but at least, now, you have begun! And you'll have the truthful answer when people ask you: "Are you a writer...?

46460546R00094

Made in the USA
Middletown, DE
30 May 2019